P9-CQC-262

"I wish you'd told me about him."

Josie was sitting on the porch swing, praying he'd gone. At the sound of his voice, she stiffened. "What do you mean?" She knew Chase was talking about her son. All night he had been making leading comments. "Look, Mr. Fowler, I don't know what you're implying. Why should I have to tell you anything?" The simmering look she saw on his face now was the same as the one he'd worn that night four years ago. "If you're talking about that night…Well, what we did has nothing to do with J.T.—"

"Sugar," he interrupted, advancing toward the swing, his step sure, his eyes boring into hers. "It has everything to do with J.T."

Josie's heart twisted, and her stomach tightened. "I may have slept with you, Chase Fowler, but that doesn't give you any rights. You've got no place in my life, or my son's." She was spitting mad now, and scared to death. "J. T. Alexander is my son— not yours."

In one fluid motion, Chase was right in front of her, his arms on either side of her as his strong hands stilled the motion of the swing. His tone darkened, as did his eyes. "Want to bet?"

Dear Reader,

This month, a new "Rising Star" comes out to shine, as American Romance continues to search for the best new talent...the best new stories.

Let me introduce you to Mindy Neff. A self-proclaimed daydreamer and hopeless romantic, Mindy had been reading romances for ten years. One day her husband cut out an article about a writer's workshop and told her, "You can do this." Mindy figured if he had that much faith in her, then she ought to give it a shot. So she set about writing the stories she loved to read, stories that touch the heart, tug at the reader's emotions and always, without fail, have a happy ending. *A Family Man*, her very first published novel, is such a story.

Turn the page and catch a Rising Star!

Regards,

Debra Matteucci
Senior Editor & Editorial Coordinator
Harlequin Books
300 East 42nd Street
New York, NY 10017

Mindy Neff

A FAMILY MAN

Harlequin Books

TORONTO • NEW YORK • LONDON
AMSTERDAM • PARIS • SYDNEY • HAMBURG
STOCKHOLM • ATHENS • TOKYO • MILAN
MADRID • WARSAW • BUDAPEST • AUCKLAND

If you purchased this book without a cover you should be aware
that this book is stolen property. It was reported as "unsold and
destroyed" to the publisher, and neither the author nor the
publisher has received any payment for this "stripped book."

To Gene,
my real-life hero, my husband and my friend.
I love you.

ISBN 0-373-16644-3

A FAMILY MAN

Copyright © 1996 by Melinda Neff.

All rights reserved. Except for use in any review, the reproduction or
utilization of this work in whole or in part in any form by any electronic,
mechanical or other means, now known or hereafter invented, including
xerography, photocopying and recording, or in any information storage
or retrieval system, is forbidden without the written permission of the
publisher, Harlequin Enterprises Limited, 225 Duncan Mill Road,
Don Mills, Ontario, Canada M3B 3K9.

All characters in this book have no existence outside the imagination of
the author and have no relation whatsoever to anyone bearing the same
name or names. They are not even distantly inspired by any individual
known or unknown to the author, and all incidents are pure invention.

This edition published by arrangement with Harlequin Books S.A.

® and TM are trademarks of the publisher. Trademarks indicated with
® are registered in the United States Patent and Trademark Office, the
Canadian Trade Marks Office and in other countries.

Printed in U.S.A.

Prologue

Desperation clawed at her, emotions so fierce she thought she'd break under their weight. She wanted to scream, stamp her feet, cry out at the injustice...shake her fist at God.

Lightning streaked the sky, creasing the inky darkness of the backwoods road. The clap of thunder that followed shook the car like an explosion, making her heart pound in both fear and repentance.

She shouldn't have run. She shouldn't be out in this storm. But the entire fabric of her life had begun to unravel today, shaking her faith, twisting her insides into knots of hopelessness. *Oh, God. Why now? Why me? Why Bobby?*

Anger, despair and crushing guilt assailed her. She'd never allowed herself to go this far, to truly let her anger consume her this way.

One thing. Just one little thing. That's all she was asking for. A tiny seed. A miracle that so many people took for granted. That *she'd* taken for granted.

Until today.

Until the horrible, final judgment, handed down
by a dispassionate doctor, had shattered her world.
Words. A death sentence. The imminent end of a
beautiful, cherished dream. A beautiful life. *Bobby's* life.

"Oh, God, please," she cried silently. If only there
was a way. She wasn't asking for herself—but for
Bobby, for the one thing he most wanted.

Driving rain slashed against the windshield, the
wipers barely able to keep up with the torrent.

Fierce, angry lightning burst from the heavens, il-
luminating the country road as if it were high noon
instead of close to midnight. A flash of hope. Gone
in an instant. Like her dreams. Like Bobby's dreams.

And then she saw the stranger.

Her heart lurched so hard she felt an instant of
vertigo. Her foot eased off the gas pedal, the car
creeping to a mere crawl.

He stood in the shadows, cloaked in darkness, no
hat, no umbrella, a lone force whose strength alone
could withstand the storm.

An explosive, rash idea, born of despair—and of
love—took hold and grew. A lifetime of caution, of
always doing the right thing, urged her to press the
accelerator and run for her very life. Yet something
else ruled her actions.

She didn't allow herself to consider the risk. She
only considered the consequences.

Brake lights splashed a crimson glow across rain-
drenched asphalt as the car rolled to a stop. She
gripped the steering wheel with damp palms, her
body so tense she ached. It could have been hours or

mere seconds. Time lost all meaning. *Get in,* she prayed silently. *Please, just get in. Let it be right.*

At last, the passenger door opened. The dome light shone like a spotlight in an interrogation room, giving her just enough time to doubt her sanity.

She stared straight ahead as his weight settled into the seat next to her. She couldn't look at him. Not yet. Not when her mind was so consumed with the enormity of what she'd just done, what she was about to *ask.*

The smell of expensive leather assailed her. A bomber jacket, she noted, the kind worn by jet jockeys in the popular air force movies.

Without speaking she eased her foot off the brake and drove on, heading into the storm. A storm created by nature and of her own emotions.

She was smart enough to realize that the rationalizations flipping one right after another through her mind were born of despair, yet a small, hopeful part of her grasped onto one repetitious thought.

Fate seemed to have thrown this man in her path. It must be right, she thought.

It had to be.

Four sinful, desperate words were rehearsed over and over in her mind, yet they remained choked in her throat. Fear robbed her voice like those long ago nights as a child, wanting desperately to call out to her mama, but so afraid that the actual sound of her voice would alert the monsters who were lurking just outside the door. Those same feelings of helpless silence once again assailed her.

He might have been battling his own demons, for he hadn't spoken in the ten miles or so they'd traveled. If she didn't act soon, she'd lose her nerve. The opportunity was here. Serendipity. An open door that held a tiny spark of hope.

She heard the rustle of his clothing and knew that he'd turned to look at her as she pulled into the parking lot of the small motel.

Perspiration slicked her palms. Staring straight ahead, she turned off the ignition. "Make love to me," she whispered at last.

Silence seemed to stretch for an eon. She knew he was watching her.

She nearly called back her words, but desperation drove her forward. Dropping her hands from the steering wheel, she turned to face him. His eyes were steady, haunting, as if he too were weighted down by sadness, a bleak sadness that should never, ever be borne alone.

"Please, just say you will. One night is all I'm asking."

The impact of his probing gaze caused her heart to trip and stumble, yet she held his look. *Don't think,* she cautioned herself. *Fate takes care of itself. If not . . .*

Rain drummed on the roof of the car. For an instant, the stern lines of his face gentled. He never uttered a word, yet with his sharp gaze locked onto hers, he acquiesced by the barest nod of his head.

She let out a trembling breath and closed her eyes.

Destiny had just charted its course.

By unspoken agreement, she waited in the car while he registered in the lobby, then taking only her keys, she followed him to the room.

He switched on a lamp by the bed, then turned to face her. For a wild moment, she wanted to bolt. She felt awkward and conspicuous and scared. Drops of rain slid down his temples. With strong fingers, he smoothed his midnight hair straight back from his forehead, then removed his leather jacket.

She remained frozen by the door, so very unsure.

He was a tall man with eyes that seemed to see clear into her soul. He must have sensed her indecision, yet he came toward her. Stopping just a bare pace from her, he cocked one dark brow.

"It's your call, sugar. Tell me what you want."

His voice was low and gravelly...sexy. It sent chills up her spine. She couldn't allow herself to become swept away like this. She had one purpose only.

"No words," she whispered.

She could almost see the questions he wanted to ask, questions she could never answer. All she wanted was one tiny seed of hope...of life.

Once again he acknowledged her wishes with a single, slight nod of his head, then slowly reached out, holding her with his eyes, giving her all that she'd asked for and more—tenderly, reverently, as if he knew her secrets...her fragility...her desperate, haunting despair...and hope.

Wind-driven rain tapped a fierce staccato against the windowpanes, but it was nothing compared to the tempest created within the small motel room.

He was a fantasy lover, gentle yet masterful, always considerate. She'd never been brought to such fulfillment, not just once, but time and again throughout the long night.

As dawn crept over the horizon, she watched him as he slept. Her hand trembled as she reached out to touch the dark hair that fell over his brow. It was a featherlight touch of gratitude. Of goodbye.

With a sense of reluctance that shamed her, she gathered her clothes and silently slipped from the room.

She didn't even know his name.

She wanted it that way.

Chapter One

The yellow, pointy nose of the AT 502 Turbine Air Tractor angled downward like a hound hot on the scent of a fox. The Mercedes of the bug bombers, Chase lovingly called the plane. Cupped wheels made contact with the short, bumpy runway. He shook his head at the sad state of disrepair of the landing strip, but it didn't affect his thistledown landing. It might be a big old plane, but Chase knew he could set her down just about anywhere.

From the side door canopy, he noticed mechanics and pilots alike had stopped what they were doing to watch him come in. He didn't blame them. It was almost as big a thrill to stand on the ground watching these ag planes perform as to fly them. The wind whistling in the spray booms almost covered the soft whine of the turbine and idling prop as he hauled the plane around and backtracked what little turf he'd used to land. Off to the side of the hangar, he neatly maneuvered the plane within reach of the loader truck.

Steady nerves, steady hands and good judgment. Chase wasn't modest. He knew he was the best.

He climbed out over the canopy sill and removed his helmet. Sweat dripped from his temples and down the back of his shirt as he finger-combed his short, dark hair.

"She's all yours, Bubba. Treat her like a lady."

"Ain't no other way, boss." Bubba Simpson touched the wing of the bright yellow plane as if indeed she were a fine lady. Bubba was the only other pilot besides himself that Chase trusted to fly the quarter-million-dollar turbine.

The two men were the same age, thirty-two, and had gone to school together over in the next parish. Bubba hadn't hesitated a minute when Chase had asked him to relocate to Alexander. Business was good, work was steady, and the financial hold Chase had been slowly gaining in this town guaranteed both his *and* Bubba's future.

"Kid hanging around over there's looking for a job," Bubba said as he ducked under the plane's belly and ran his hand over the prop.

Chase saw the guy—young, he noted—pacing outside the hangar, hands stuffed in the back pockets of his jeans like a kid who was dying to touch but had been threatened with dire consequences if he did.

He grinned. That young man had *pilot* written all over him. They were a certain breed he could spot a mile off.

As much as Chase loved to fly, he could sorely use a couple more pilots. He was right in the middle of his busiest season and he had more acres under contract to spray than he and Bubba could handle on their own.

In addition to his ag work, the airstrip needed minor repairs and the house needed a major face lift . . . and *somewhere* in amongst all this, there was a little family matter that needed tending to. A question he figured it was high time he got an answer to. A thirty-two-year-old question.

Heading toward the crude office that was fashioned off to one side of the hangar, Chase noticed that the painters had done their job. A sign above the bay doors of the hangar read: Fowler's Flying Service. He liked the look of it. He especially liked the name. He figured it was about time somebody else's name was touted about town besides the Alexanders'. Yeah, he thought, just seeing his name up there in big letters made the eighteen-hour workdays go down a little easier.

He stopped in front of the lanky kid, in his early twenties he guessed. "Chase Fowler." He extended his hand. "Help you with something?"

"Name's Junior Watkins. Heard you were looking for ag pilots."

"Maybe. Come on inside."

He noticed how Junior's eyes kept straying to the turbine as Bubba readied it for takeoff. Chase laughed. "Don't get your hopes up, kid. So far, nobody flies that baby but Bubba and me." Chase fed quarters into the Coke machine and extracted two bottles, handing one to Junior.

"Man, she is a honey. How does she handle?"

"Takes some getting used to." Chase shifted papers on his cluttered desk and rested one hip against the edge. "Sort of like having power steering. Nothing at all like horsing the 301's around where it takes two hands on the stick to turn. Rudder's easier, too. After thirteen hours on the tach, my knees appreciate the hell out of it.''

''I'd sure like to give her a try sometime.''

''We might be getting ahead of ourselves here. Why don't I tell you what I'm looking for and you can tell me if you're qualified.''

''Fair enough.''

The irony of his own words wasn't lost on Chase. He believed in letting people speak for themselves— but somehow no one in this town had ever let his qualifications speak for him. In Alexander, Louisiana, only the Alexanders were heard. Chase nodded, his eyes steely. Yes, he'd been obsessing on this lately, on his past. He'd been consumed by it. But, he thought as he took a swig of Coke, that was about to change. Chase Fowler was about to speak—and soon everyone in this town would hear him. No one, or nothing, would stand in his way.

CHASE WAS IN A HURRY, which was a lame excuse for nearly mowing down the lady coming in the opposite direction on the sidewalk.

''My apologies, ma'am.'' Quick thinking and a sure grip were the only things that kept the woman on her feet.

''No. My fault. I'm sorry. I wasn't looking wh—'' Her gaze lifted and she froze.

And so did Chase. A distant memory slammed into his gut, rendering him immobile.

He hadn't expected ever to see this woman again.

''I remember you,'' he drawled. It'd been close to four years, but he could've called up her image any time, day or night. He'd done it more times than he cared to admit. The part that had eaten at him, though, was that he didn't even have a name to go with the vivid face and erotic memories.

Man, she'd been incredible. It had been strange, meeting up with her like that. He'd been on his way back from Dallas, picking up a plane, when the oil gauge had gone haywire forcing him to set the Cessna down on an old service road next to a field. He hadn't figured on hitching a ride with a dark-haired beauty whose eyes were filled with sadness and desperation. A desperation that had pretty much matched his own that night.

Those green eyes held a similar look just now. Chase couldn't figure it. He didn't normally arouse this particular reaction in women.

"Don't tell me you don't remember me, sugar."

"No." Her gaze skittered away. "I don't recall—"

"Yes, you do," he interrupted softly. He saw her green eyes close, saw the fine trembling of her fisted hands. "There's no way two people could do what we did in that motel room and forget about it. At least not in this lifetime. Why'd you run away?"

She shook her head, holding her hands out as if to ward off a blow. "Get away from me," she whispered, her eyes flitting up and down the street. "I told you, I've never seen you before." She looked around as if the glass-front buildings and concrete sidewalks had ears.

She made an attempt to shoot by him, but Chase caught her arm. "Wait. At least give me your name." He'd be damned if he'd let her slip away a second time. At least not without knowing her name. Four years was a long time to be tortured by fantasies.

"Just . . . just leave me alone."

The fear and genuine distress in her widened eyes and trembling mouth made Chase rein hard on his control. "Just a name, sugar. You owe me that much."

A spark of defiance overshadowed the fear. He noted it and admired it. This woman had fire. God, did she have fire.

"I don't owe you anything."

He saw the faint pink of her cheeks and realized his words had sounded crude, so he switched tactics. "You're right. Never mind. It'd probably be just as easy to ask around, this being a small town and all. 'Course the fine folks of Alexander, Louisiana'd probably start speculating, and then they'd want to know why I wanted to know, and then I'd have to come up with something to tell them, and you *know* how nasty these gossip mills can be, and—"

"Josie."

Ah, sometimes an alternate course was all it took. He smiled. "Josie, what?"

"Alexander."

That wiped the smile right off his face. His stomach lurched and rolled, a sensation very similar to the one he experienced when flying wingovers in his crop duster. All thoughts of teasing her into good humor fled.

"One of *the* Alexanders?" he asked, praying she'd deny it so he wouldn't feel as if he'd committed a mortal sin. "Like the town?"

For some reason that particular question got her back up. Her shoulders straightened and her spine went rigid, as if an unseen hand had just jerked an invisible string attached to the top of her head. She was fairly tall, about five-eight, he'd guess, and most of that height was in her legs. He had a hard time keeping his mind on the questions at hand and off those long, lean legs. Just the memory of what they felt like wrapped around him caused his brain to stall.

"I don't think there are any other kind around these parts," she said.

"What I meant, sugar, is do you come by that name by birth or by marriage?"

She looked as if he'd just slapped her. It was an almost tangible hurt. He had no idea why, but it made him feel like a jerk.

"Marriage."

Chase let out a long breath, but relief was not to be granted. God Almighty, he'd never slept with a married woman in his life. "Well, now, that presents a whole new set of problems and questions. Your place or mine?"

"Excuse me?"

"As it turns out, we've got a little business to discuss."

"I can't imagine any business you and I would have to discuss," she whispered fiercely. "The past is history. Just leave it alone."

"So you *do* remember me," he challenged.

"I didn't say—"

Just then, a woman—whose hair Chase could have sworn was blue—poked her head out the door of the beauty shop and drawled, "Josie Mae, ya'll want to come on inside where it's cool? I can pour you kids a nice cold glass of Coca-Cola. Lordy, it's a hot one today. And sticky."

"No, thank you, Miss Vira," she called.

"Are you sure, hon? It'd be no trouble."

"No, ma'am. I need to get on home."

Her startling green eyes were wide, her smile forced. Josie Alexander was hiding something and fairly itching to get away from him. Hell, wasn't that just like his luck. This whole damned town was full of secrets. Most of them revolving smack dab around his own.

He'd moved in a week ago, intending to steer clear of anyone with the last name of Alexander—at least until his financial position in the community was so firmly entrenched that he could snub his nose at their brand of small town prejudice.

It appeared he'd already broken his own code. Four years ago. On a rainy night. In a low budget motel.

With Josie Mae Alexander.

The lady with blue hair was still watching them with avid fascination. He figured he might as well go introduce himself to the local beauty shop owner. It was a guaranteed way to make sure his name was passed along with record speed. Sometimes small town gossip had its merits. Within about fifteen minutes, speculation would be rife. He just hoped that speculation reached the right ears.

"Afternoon, ma'am. Name's Chase Fowler." Though he'd relayed the information to the beauty shop owner, he was more interested in the impact it had on Josie Alexander. He noted that he'd caught her off guard. He also noted that she'd made the connection. Good.

"You're new around these parts, aren't you?" Vira asked.

"Yes, ma'am. Just bought the old Alexander place up the road a piece. Gonna put that airstrip to good use with my dusters."

"Why, I declare. You and Josie Mae are neighbors. Did you know that, Josie Mae?" Vira called, just as Josie was about to slip away.

"Why, no, Miss Vira, I sure didn't." She gave another forced smile and edged away. "I've really got to run now. Ya'll take care."

This time Chase didn't bother to stop her departure. Escape was more like it, he decided as he watched the sway of her slim hips beneath her modest shorts. The slap of her sandals against the hot pavement were a dead give away to both her agitation and her hurry.

"We'll meet again, Mrs. Alexander," he warned silently.

JOSIE SAT ON THE PORCH, gripping an ice-cold glass of lemonade. Her heart alternately raced and throbbed, making her feel sick to her stomach. Dusk wasn't far off. It should have been a peaceful time of day, when the sun no longer beat down like flames from hell, but any hope of serenity had been shattered that afternoon.

Chase Fowler.

The one man who could blow her carefully built world sky-high.

Fate, she thought. She'd accepted it four years ago, welcomed it with both terror and anticipation. She chafed against it now.

She closed her eyes for a moment and rolled the icy glass across her forehead. Rainbirds chugged in a soothing rhythm across the yard, leaving beads of water clinging to the blades of grass. This familiar sound should have relaxed her, but the events of the afternoon prevented the calm she sought.

Sooner or later Chase would show up. She knew that as surely as she knew the boll weevils would eat at the cotton. She had something that belonged to him, and it was a great deal more than just the property assessment paper the attorneys had forgotten to forward. She'd told them it was no problem. Since the new owner lived so close, she'd just drop it off herself.

That had been before she'd known who Chase Fowler was.

Oh, God, what now? The sins of her past were about to come back and condemn her. Avoiding him would buy her time, time to think, to plan. But she couldn't hide forever.

She couldn't hide her son.

Barefoot, she stepped off the porch and shut off the Rainbirds, then went to the side yard where another sprinkler made slow, back and forth passes over the yard. Tugging the hose, she positioned the stream of water, making sure it reached the bed of impatiens and lilies she'd lovingly planted along the edge of the house.

She glanced over at J.T., who was engrossed in making what she supposed were truck noises as he pushed his toy fire engine around in the dirt.

"J.T.," she called, cursing silently when her voice wobbled. "Want to go with Mama around back and check on the cows?"

The toddler popped up. "Moo cows," he squealed, pumping his little arms and legs as he hurried to reach her side. Lord, how she loved this baby. Scooping him up, she held him close and pressed her lips against his soft cheek. Unaccountably, tears welled in her eyes and her throat began to ache. The emotions steamrolling through her at that moment were almost more than she could contain.

J.T. began to wriggle, so she set him down. Before his feet had even touched the ground, his attention was snared by a butterfly resting on a dandelion. He leapt, startling the beautiful insect into flight, then shrieked in the carefree glee so typical of a child and gave chase.

Any other time, Josie would have laughed at his antics. But not today. If she allowed herself to laugh, the hysteria she was trying so desperately to hold at bay might escape.

As they made their way toward the south pasture, J.T. skipped along beside her, oblivious to the turmoil clawing like a beast at her insides.

It wore her out just watching him, his energy, his blessed, carefree innocence. Every once in a while he'd trip over his own feet or a stubborn weed. He'd fall flat on his face like a sack of flour. Each time it happened, Josie's immediate reaction was to rush to his side and coddle. But J.T. had a determined, independent streak that wouldn't quit. He'd just giggle, pop back up and continue on at full speed, leaving Josie's heartbeat in a continual flux of stop and start.

The worrying was both natural and universal, though her best friend, Mary Alice, had chided her on more than one occasion that she was just a tad overprotective. Josie didn't agree. Her first and foremost mission as a mother was to protect her baby at all costs. She'd always thought of him as her miracle child. A precious gift she cherished more than her own life.

She'd do anything to keep him safe.

Anything.

Checking to make sure J.T. stayed clear of the thorny blackberry bush, Josie flipped the garden hose over the edge of the trough. Using the top half of a weathered bleach bottle, she skimmed green slime off the water's surface and tossed it over the sagging fence.

As she waited for the water level in the trough to rise, she breathed deep, hoping the tranquil sounds and smells of the farm would lull her, ease the clenching fear and uncertainty that weighed on her chest like a hot, heavy rock. The crickets were singing in the grass, harmonizing with the cicadas. Their evening song changed in tempo a bare instant before J.T.'s little voice rang out.

"Airplane!"

Josie looked past the barn, across the expanse of cotton as a bright yellow, single-engine plane swooped in low for a landing.

The whine of the engine was a familiar sound she'd been hearing since childhood. Tonight, it created within her a wealth of anxiety.

Her time of reckoning was almost at hand.

When she'd sold the adjacent property with its abandoned airstrip, she'd thought it would herald the beginning of her freedom. With the money from the sale, she'd been able to pay off the rest of the past due medical bills.

The whole transaction had taken place by phone and mail through the attorney over in Monroe. She'd known the buyer's name, but not his face.

A face from her past.

A stranger she'd known in the most intimate way for only a few brief hours.

Chase Fowler.

Oh, God. She'd told herself that destiny had put him in her path that night four years ago, a night when desperation had ruled her thoughts and actions. Now, she had to face the very real fear that the destiny she'd clung to so fiercely might very well turn what happened on that rainy night into a custody battle.

CHASE KNOCKED ON THE DOOR of the farmhouse, but got no answer. A dust coated Bronco was parked in the carport. He hoped to God it wasn't her husband's. He told himself he had a legitimate reason for being here—he was just saving her a trip to deliver the land document that had inadvertently been left out of the escrow package.

And if he believed that, he was lying through his teeth.

When he knocked again without any response, he turned—and came to a dead stop.

Josie stood by the corner of the house, her attention divided between him and something around the corner. As it had that afternoon, the sight of her poleaxed him. God, she was beautiful. Firm, tanned legs stretched from beneath denim shorts. Her long, dark hair was caught up off her neck in deference to the heat, several stray tendrils clinging to the perspiration on her nape.

"Evenin', Miz Alexander," he drawled in a good-ol'-boy accent, surprised at how nervous he felt now that he was actually here, facing her again. "Small world, huh?"

He saw her chin lift, saw her sweet green eyes dart away, as if she were hiding something just around the corner of the house.

"Evidently."

"Who'd have thought we'd be neighbors? Makes me wonder if you'd have sold that property if you'd known the buyer."

"I knew."

"Hmm. I don't recall exchanging names." He vividly recalled her whispered plea of "no words."

"Mr. Fowler—"

"Chase," he interrupted. "With the history between us, seems a mite silly to call me Mister."

Her chin raised with her inhaled breath. "I needed the money that airstrip brought, you obviously needed the land. We both got what we wanted, so why don't we leave it at that? I make it a point not to dwell on the past or what-ifs . . . Mr. Fowler."

"Mama! Mama!"

The sound of the child's voice jolted Chase like the blast of a shotgun, making him realize just how futile this visit was. How his attraction for this woman would have to be ignored. She said she'd gotten her name through marriage, but he'd held out a slim, morbid hope that she was divorced.

The little kid narrowed that possibility considerably.

Chase would never stoop to becoming a home wrecker. He had firsthand experience of what that could do to a kid, to a family. It went against the moral code he prided himself on.

He understood his own shock, his disappointment. What he didn't get was the obvious nervousness and the hint of genuine fear that Josie Alexander was trying so hard to hide. And failing miserably.

He looked beyond her to the little boy he could now see dawdling by the azalea bush, trying his best to pounce on a reluctant frog. The dark haired tot looked up, obviously realized they had company, and came barreling around the side of the house, throwing himself against the front of Josie's legs with the kind of trust only a child clings to.

She cupped the back of the little boy's head, looking as if she wanted to snatch him up and run screaming in the opposite direction.

The picture didn't fit.

The feeling that something wasn't right, that she was hiding something, began to grow stronger in Chase, taking shape like a newly planted bush of cotton after a gentle rain.

The child finally lifted his head from where he'd tucked it in the crease of his mother's legs and shyly glanced at Chase.

Sheer speechlessness jolted him.

His jaw clenched and his muscles tightened as he stared at the little boy. Shape, color and size, the eyes confronting him from the miniature face were a mirror image of his own.

"Well, I'll be damned." His gaze traveled back to Josie's face—a face he'd dreamed about often. She looked about as shell-shocked as he felt, reminding him a bit of a rabbit who was frozen in the deadly, hypnotic path of a cobra. Well, damn it, he had a right to strike. He didn't make a habit of strewing offspring around the four corners of Louisiana, and unless he had a twin roaming the state, there was a very real possibility that this was his child.

Chapter Two

J.T., in his limited years, didn't sense the emotional storm brewing between the two adults. "Hi!" he chirped. Although the greeting was outgoing, he still kept a prudent hold on Josie's leg.

Chase knelt down eye level with the little boy, searching the miniature blue eyes. His entire world felt off-kilter. Could this be his son?

"Hello there, sport."

"I'm not Sport! I'm J.T.!"

"J.T., hmm? Can you say your whole name?"

"Yep. Mama teached it to me." He puffed out his stocky little chest. "James Troy Aw-wig-zn'dr. Right, Mama?" He looked up at Josie for approval.

"That's right, sweetie."

Encouraged, J.T. seemed intent on showing off. "And I'm dis many," he said, proudly holding up three stubby fingers.

"Three whole years?" Chase said. "You're quite a little man."

"Yep."

Josie's heart pounded so hard she began to feel dizzy. She needed control. Needed to throw him off the scent he seemed so determined to track. Stop the disastrous snowball before their lives ended up more entwined than she could ever allow.

"We named him after his great-grandfather," she inserted, reminding him that there was another man to be considered. She was, after all, *Mrs*. Alexander.

"Grandfather," Chase corrected.

"Excuse me?"

A slow grin creased his cheeks, yet his blue eyes, eyes so like her son's, held an edge of caution. "My dad's name is James."

Josie felt as if she'd fallen down the rabbit hole or been caught in a time warp. Life just didn't hold this many coincidences.

"I meant Bobby's grandfather," she mumbled.

He raised a brow, but she could see a subtle tension around his full mouth. "Bobby, hmm? That'd be the husband. I knocked when I came up, but nobody answered. Suppose this conversation should be discussed between the three of us?"

Josie shook her head, unsure of how to head him off. Sooner or later he'd find out about Bobby. All he had to do was ask around town.

"Look, I really don't want to mess up your life here, or your marriage, but I've got a lot of questions." His vivid blue eyes nearly seared her with their intense gaze. Quietly he said, "I think I have a right to some answers."

Answers were one thing she didn't want to give Chase Fowler. She was more than afraid of his questions. Did he notice how much J.T. resembled him, and realize the boy was his son?

"You're assuming an awful lot based on a single encounter," she hissed, careful to keep her voice steady and low so J.T. wouldn't hear. She didn't have to worry on that score. J.T. was already scrambling off after the frog.

"It was one hell of an incredible encounter, lady. That little catch in your voice and the way those green eyes of yours keep wandering over my jeans tells me your memory's just as good as mine."

He stood, bringing all six foot two of virile masculinity into perfect view. Josie's entire being reacted to that aggressive stance. She knew what his dark hair felt like slipping through her fingers, recalled the way his skin stretched taut over his high cheek bones during the height of arousal, the way his mouth could tip with the barest hint of amusement one second and administer mind shattering pleasure the next. His chest, hidden now beneath a light cotton shirt, was strong and wide, his belly washboard flat. And his thighs were so very powerful and erotic, like his sex.

Oh, God. What in the world was she thinking? A wave of shame heated her skin. She scooped J.T. into her arms and walked toward the porch steps.

"Excuse me. I need to give J.T. a bath."

Chase blocked her way and laid a hand on her arm. Invisible sparks shot all the way up her shoulder and across her breasts, tightening them beneath the snug tank top.

"Running, Josie? You're good at that. But I won't go away. I want some answers."

"Not now."

"Is your husband due home soon? Is that it?"

Josie shook her head and edged toward the door. He let her go. The fact that he did caused her to pause. She didn't want to answer his questions. How could she explain to him that Bobby wouldn't be coming home? Not now. Not ever. Her childhood sweetheart, the guy who'd been her best friend in all the world had died six days before J.T. was born. It didn't quite seem fair that Bobby was gone and that Chase was standing here on her porch, a specter from the past, very alive and very vital.

Memories of the dark stranger had surfaced throughout the years, causing a guilt she'd been hard-pressed to hide. That one impulsive decision to sleep with a stranger had haunted her days. And nights.

Impulsive or not, her heart had been in the right place, she'd assured herself over and over throughout the years. She'd loved Bobby, would have moved heaven and earth to give him what he wanted. And what he'd wanted most was a baby. Their baby. In the end he hadn't lived to even hold J.T.

Josie was human enough to admit she had some regrets, but she'd never regretted the baby. Or the joy her pregnancy had brought to her husband. She consoled herself that he had died in peace, happy that a part of his life would live on, through their son. The baby had meant so much to both of them. She didn't consider what she'd done an act of adultery. It had been an act of love. Love for Bobby.

She wouldn't tarnish or betray that memory, no matter what emotions that one night of passion stirred in her.

"Josie?" he prompted softly.

"I'm a widow, Chase. My husband died."

A strange look came over his face, one she couldn't decipher. Given the state of her own emotions, she didn't have the energy to dwell on that haunted expression.

He didn't budge when she opened the screen door. Short of bodily throwing him off her property, which she had to admit was a ridiculous notion, there wasn't much she could do. Despite his laid-back demeanor, he struck her as a man who didn't give up easily.

Josie sighed. "You can stay or you can go, but right now I've got to take care of my son."

As invitations went, that one was certainly ungracious, but Chase figured he'd take what he could get. Letting himself in through the screen door, which moments ago had banged in his face, he stopped just inside the living room to look around. The old farmhouse was spacious. He'd expected opulence—hell, she was an Alexander wasn't she? Instead, he encountered simple country charm. Some of the furnishings looked like antiques, but not the showy, priceless kind he'd expect a rich bitch to own.

Which went to show that he was jumping to a lot of conclusions. The biggest one was whether that little boy in there was his son.

Over the fireplace mantel stood a grouping of photographs. With more anticipation than he'd like to admit, Chase went to study them. He looked at the picture closest to him. Josie, pregnant and smiling into the face of a man. Chase's jaw clenched, and as he picked up the frame, his knuckles whitened from the tense grip he held it in. So this was Bobby. Finally he saw what the man looked like. He looked older than Chase, but it was hard to tell. The guy was way too thin, his skin pale. His eyes were shining though, happy, gazing with indisputable love at the woman whose arms were wrapped securely around his thin frame. Chase's chest tightened, with an undefinable emotion. Was it envy?

"That was Bobby."

Chase nearly jumped at the sound of her voice. Carefully, he placed the picture back on the mantel and turned around. "How'd he die?"

"Leukemia. He had a rough time in the end, but Bobby never let anything—not even death—get him down. He was always so positive, so up. Sometimes I think it was *his* strength that kept me going rather than the other way around."

Chase had a hard time keeping his mind on her quiet words. His mind kept conjuring the face of the man in the photo. "You loved him," he stated.

"Very much."

"Then why—?"

"Don't. Not now, Chase. Please."

Chase looked at the pajama clad little boy she clutched so protectively in her arms. She was right. Now wasn't the time to get into the whys and wherefores of a one-night stand. Besides, she'd just used his given name and the sound of it rolling off her tongue in that smoky, almost fearful voice did something to his insides. He inclined his head, letting her know she'd won this round and watched as she visibly relaxed.

She tried to set J.T. down, but the boy was tired and cranky. He started to fuss and cling to her.

"J.T., honey, don't you want to play with your trucks so Mama can get supper?"

"No!" He whimpered and clung harder.

"Will he let me hold him?"

Josie looked at Chase. Her nerves were stretched to the breaking point. She had an irrational fear that if she handed J.T. over to this man, she might not ever get him back. It was a dumb thought. And right about now she could use an extra pair of hands. J.T. was a strong-willed child and as tired as he was, she knew he'd kick up a ruckus if she put him down.

She shrugged, but stood still as Chase approached. "He probably will. This kid's not afraid of anybody and he likes to get his own way." *Just like someone else I'm coming to know,* she thought.

Chase held out his arms and J.T. fairly jumped into them. "There you go, sport. Let's let your mama get you a meal."

Josie had to turn away. The sight of the two dark heads so close together caused a lump to form in her chest. J.T. was hers. He had been from the beginning and she didn't want to share him.

Hoping a little distance would ease her inner turmoil, Josie headed for the kitchen. J.T. might be an amiable little boy, but he wouldn't be distracted for long.

The bread was still warm from the oven and the soup steaming since it had been simmering most of the day. It was a meal better suited for a cold rainy night rather than the hot muggy heat of June, but she'd needed to use up the leftovers before they spoiled.

Reaching for bowls and silverware, Josie hesitated. She could hear J.T.'s high-pitched giggle coming from the next room, as well as the deep rumble of a masculine voice. Country manners dictated that she offer Chase Fowler a meal. It was the right and proper thing to do, and Josie had always been known to do the *right* thing. *Smile, Josie. You're a good girl, Josie. You mustn't make waves, Josie. Do such and such, Josie, or folks will talk.*

Well, she'd certainly done something that'd make folks talk. How in the world would she ever survive a scandal the likes of what Chase's presence could very well create?

She turned when Chase carried J.T. into the kitchen. His brow raised in a silent question as he glanced toward the extra place setting. It was just a simple look, Josie told herself. A quirk of the brow. An expression. There wasn't any call for the way her stomach and heart exchanged places, the way every body part from north to south went all fluttery.

"We're having leftovers—a stew of sorts. Nothing fancy." Her words sounded like an apology so she shut her mouth. Plucking J.T. from his arms, she strapped him into the wooden high chair and snapped the tray in place.

Chase sat down at the table, caught a little off guard. He hadn't expected her to invite him to supper. Judging by her actions so far, he wondered if he ought to check his bowl for arsenic. He watched Josie hurry around the kitchen, tying a bib around J.T.'s neck, pouring milk into a Micky Mouse cup with a plastic lid.

She didn't look like a woman who belonged on a farm. Although he didn't normally go for stereotyping, he found himself thinking that she didn't strike him as the typical image he had of a mother, either. Her nails were manicured and polished, not a jagged edge in sight. Her skin had a dewy, healthy glow as if she'd spent a day at a fancy salon. A skillful blending of shadow made her green eyes exotic, her cheekbones prominent. Her full lips were glossy with color, sending his imagination into orbit.

As she stretched to get ice cubes out of the freezer, Chase nearly groaned aloud. More than anything, he wanted to go to her, slip his arms around her trim waist and press himself against that firm derriere. God Almighty, he remembered the shape and feel of that bottom—as well as every other square inch of her from top to toe. The memories made him hot.

It'd be wise to focus his attention elsewhere, he decided, like on the mess little James Troy was making out of a slice of buttered bread.

"Wouldn't it have made better sense to bathe him after he ate?"

Josie handed J.T. a child size spoon, then placed two steaming bowls of stew on the table. "That's what the bib's for. Besides, he's pretty tuckered out. I'll be lucky if he stays awake through supper."

Chase tasted the stew. Leftovers or not, the lady could cook. "This is good. Thank you." He noticed that she mainly toyed with her meal. The child, on the other hand, was digging in. It awed Chase just to watch the little boy. The enthusiasm, the energy, the pleased grin upon making a new discovery, no matter how small. He'd never really yearned for domesticity or fatherhood, yet he suddenly found the prospect exciting. Frankly, it scared him how much he hoped this little boy was actually born of his genes.

"He wields that spoon pretty good."

Josie smiled and reached over to wipe a stray piece of carrot off J.T.'s chin. "He's always been highly coordinated. People often mistake his age because he talks so well."

That didn't surprise Chase. He'd been a gifted child himself. "He comes by it rightly."

He saw her stiffen and decided to give her a break. A cornered animal would usually hurt itself rather than give up, or come out fighting against impossible odds. He didn't want Josie in that position. He wanted her gentled so she'd open up to him.

They finished the meal in silence. As she'd predicted, J.T. was practically falling asleep in his plate. When Josie had him cleaned up and announced her intention to put him to bed, Chase stood. "Mind if I tag along?"

He saw the immediate protest she wanted to voice. Noticed, too, the weary set to her shoulders, the darkening circles forming under her eyes. Finally, she shrugged, as if she just didn't have the energy to fight. "Suit yourself."

He did, and followed her through the house.

"Man alive, this is something." His enthusiasm was genuine as he entered the little boy's room. The walls were papered with airplanes, just about every conceivable model. Toys were sticking out of an old crate that had been decorated with decals of monster trucks and more airplanes. The crib and dresser were of sturdy maple. It was a room right out of his deepest childhood fantasies.

"Look at this." He moved forward to take a closer look at the wallpaper. "There's even an old 450 Stearman."

"J.T.'s crazy over planes." Josie smiled at the baby who had one hand wound in her hair, his thumb stuck in his mouth. "And trucks and tractors—actually anything mechanical." She shifted him on her hip and jiggled the crib railing in an effort to lower it. The grip she had on J.T.'s pajama shirt pulled the material off his shoulder.

Everything within Chase went still at what he saw.

All night he'd been wondering about this baby's paternity, admittedly playing possum with Josie, taunting her and gauging her reaction. Well, he thought, as he felt his blood pump with renewed vengeance, he didn't need to bluff anymore.

The proof was staring him straight in the face.

JOSIE STRUGGLED with the crib railing, yanking at it without success. The spring mechanism was sticking again, as usual. She felt Chase move up behind her, felt his heat, the touch of his hand at her waist. She was so rattled, she nearly dropped her son.

"Here, let me help."

"Thanks." She cleared her throat and stepped back. "He's really outgrown the crib, but I haven't had a chance to haul the regular bed down from the attic."

"I'll get it down for you tomorrow."

"No, that's—"

He glanced up at her with a look that spoke of determination. "The spring on this crib has had it. I'll get the bed down tomorrow."

For just an instant, there was something so intense in his deep blue eyes, she had an urge to wrap her arms around her son and run for her very life. Lord, she must be more distraught than she'd thought. Without further argument, she allowed him to deal with the faulty spring.

With his dark head bent over his task, Josie found herself shamelessly studying him, wondering about that fleeting emotion she'd seen, an emotion that seemed to say, "you can run, little girl, but you can't hide." Her heart pumped just a little harder at the fanciful image.

Lamplight shone on his high cheekbones, accenting the hollows in his cheeks and the hint of dark stubble around his jaw. His shoulders were so broad, his hands large and capable. He ought to look out of place in her son's room, yet he didn't.

The minute she thought it, she felt like a traitor. Then the side of the crib came down with a crash and Josie jumped.

"Well, that did it. You won't be able to put it back up." Chase's voice was sharp, his words clipped, as if he'd suddenly run out of patience. "Will he be okay sleeping with the side down? If not, I've got some tools in the truck to fix it."

"No. That's okay. He's ready to be in a regular bed anyway." She'd been alone for so long, it was hard to even think about sharing the load, allowing a man to take care of all the repairs that needed doing, repairs that seemed to be piling up faster than any one person could keep up with. She found herself dreaming about the possibilities, though, then immediately chided herself for the fantasy. No matter how enticing the dream, she couldn't allow it to continue. Especially not with this man.

Chiding herself for the foolish thoughts, she eased her son into the crib. After tucking him in with a light blanket and stuffed animal, she recited a little prayer then switched off the lamp. Chase hesitated by the crib and Josie wanted to jerk him away from the bedside, insist that he leave and never come back.

But J.T. was a wonderful little boy and, as much as she hated to admit it, Chase had every right to get to know him. Could she tell him the truth, though? The repercussions of that admission would be enormous. And not just for her. For her son, too.

Feeling cooped up and restless, Josie led the way back down the hallway, through the living room and stepped out on the porch. Heat lightning flashed off in the distance.

"He's a neat kid," Chase said, his voice deep with an underlying thread of tension.

"Yes. He means the world to me." Josie turned and looked at him, then sat down on the porch swing.

"I wish you'd told me about him."

She stiffened. "What do you mean? There was nothing to tell."

"And *no one* to tell?" he taunted.

The tenuous control she had on her emotions threatened to snap. All night Chase had been making leading comments, comments that no doubt were meant to entice a reaction from her. She'd tried her

best not to take the bait but she was tired now and
her resolve was crumbling. She struggled to steel
herself. She raised her chin and looked him right in
the eye. "Look, Mr. Fowler, I don't know what
you're implying. Why should I have to tell *you* anything?" The simmering look she saw on his face now
was the same as the one he wore that night four years
ago. "If you're talking about that night... Well, I
was dealing with some pretty heavy emotions...
and what we did has nothing to do with J.T."

"Stop right there, sugar. About the only claim I
have to really knowing you is in the biblical sense.
But you don't strike me as a one-night stand
sort."

Josie was horrified by his words. They made her
feel cheap, a feeling she'd studiously avoided every
time thoughts of that night had cropped up. Her
heart twisted and her stomach tightened. She had an
idea this man was about to take her on a guided tour
of hell.

Clenching her fingers around the chain of the
porch swing, she looked at Chase, her gaze steady
and direct in contrast to the turmoil wreaking havoc
on her insides. He'd propped himself against the
wood railing, his arms folded across his chest, an-
kles crossed. For all his relaxed attitude, she knew
that he, too, was walking a very fine line.

"Bobby and I had been married for five years.
He's the only man I've ever made love with."

His brows lifted, mocking her words. "I see. You
made love with your husband and had sex with others. Then you ended up pregnant, but lucky you,
there was no one around to challenge the baby's paternity. Until I came along."

Josie wanted to slap him. She tried to put herself in his place, to understand his feelings of anger, the feelings that caused him to want to strike out. But for once in her life, she wasn't feeling a bit charitable to another human being. All thoughts of admissions or heartrending explanations scattered like seeds in the wind. She was holding all the cards. He had no proof, no basis for his assumption. As far as she was concerned, he could just go right on assuming.

"You know, I'm not usually wrong about people, but you're an exception. You're not a nice man, Chase Fowler. I don't want you anywhere near my son. I might have slept with you, but that doesn't give you any rights. You've got no place in my life, or my son's." She was spitting mad now and scared to death. "Your arrogance is beyond anything I've ever encountered. J.T. is *my* son, not yours."

"Want to bet?" His tone darkened, as did his eyes. "I can order blood tests, Josie."

"You'd put a total stranger through that? A baby, for God's sake? Why? What are you basing this obsession on? Millions of kids have dark hair and blue eyes and—" She drew in a sharp breath. "What are you doing?"

Slowly, his eyes never leaving her face, Chase had pushed himself off the railing and straightened. The buttons on his cotton shirt were now open to the waist.

Josie began to feel genuine fear.

He pulled the shirttails out of his jeans, then whipped the material off, bunching it in his hand. "This is what I'm basing it on."

The light spilling through the screen door illuminated his sculpted shoulders and torso. God help her, she didn't want to react to that male virility. Before her mind was snagged too far off course, she became aware that he was pointing to a spot on his upper shoulder. There, shining like a beacon against the night was a birthmark, the exact replica of the one J.T. had on his own tiny shoulder.

Josie felt herself trembling, but there wasn't a thing in the world she could do to stop the tremors. The crescent-shaped mark told its own story.

"Oh, God," she whispered. "This can't come out!"

Chapter Three

When he spoke again, his voice was low, raspy, strained with barely leashed control. "And if I don't see it that way?"

Josie felt a moment's fear, but she couldn't back down now. Her son's well-being—his whole future—was at stake.

"Then I'm sorry."

"You're sorry?" His brows drew low over narrowed eyes. "My son deserves to have my name, Josie."

"He has a name."

"*My* name," he stressed. "It's what I want."

"What *you* want?" Josie had an overwhelming urge to hit something. Her heart pounded and her stomach twisted. "You're not the only one involved here."

"Obviously."

"As far as I'm concerned, you were only my sperm donor." Oh, no. Now she'd admitted it and there was no turning back.

"Sperm—" He sputtered to a stop, his look thunderous. "I'm the kid's *father*. I own up to my responsibilities."

"I'm not asking you to be responsible."

"Well, that's a damned switch. Most women would, you know."

"I'm not most women." Why couldn't he see that? She sighed, feeling as if her whole life were falling apart before her eyes. She'd thought her motives were so pure and unselfish. Maybe others wouldn't see it that way, but Josie truly believed she'd acted out of love alone.

"When did Bobby die?"

The switch in subjects only increased her anxiety. What was he up to? "Why?"

"Just answer the question. Was it before or after J.T. was born?"

"Before."

He swore. "Then your sperm donor analogy won't cut it. That little boy never knew your husband, but he knows me. And he's going to know me a whole lot better."

"Chase, don't do this to me." Josie felt tears building, nearly choking her. But she refused to cry in front of him. She'd been through too much in her twenty-eight years. Vulnerabilities were to be hidden, not laid out for any and all to sneer at and take advantage of. That lesson had been learned at the hands of her own mother.

"What about me?" he asked.

"I don't know. I need some time." Josie knew she'd have to make some decisions. She also knew she wasn't in the right frame of mind to make those decisions. Once before she'd acted impulsively. It had been the only time in her life she'd veered so far off her normal course. She wouldn't make the same mistake twice.

"Fine. You take some time and think about it. I'll be back tomorrow."

"Chase—"

"I need to get that bed out of the attic."

"There's no need for you to do that."

"I'll be back," he repeated harshly and strode off the porch, his discarded shirt still clutched in his hand.

The sound of the truck's door being wrenched open and slammed shut echoed like an explosion in the night. Even the crickets and tree frogs hushed up at the disturbance. Dust and rocks flew as the tires on his pickup spun. Oh, God, she cried silently. He was madder than sin. In that state, Chase Fowler was a wild card—and Josie wasn't particularly fond of surprises. They had a way of keeping a person off-balance, never knowing whether to expect danger or triumph.

The fact that she knew very little of Chase Fowler's true personality caused a wealth of anxiety within Josie. It also made her admit something to herself that she'd been resisting with a fierce passion.

She no longer had complete and total control over the course she'd chosen for J.T.'s life, as well as her own.

Her worst nightmare had just come true.

Lightning flickered again in the clear sky. Normally she'd enjoy just sitting out here watching one of nature's dramatic light shows. But tonight she was too keyed up.

Going back in the house, she checked on J.T., relieved that he was sleeping soundly, then headed for the spare bedroom she'd turned into a workshop of sorts. She switched on her sewing machine and grabbed a precut swatch of delicate, ivory satin. If she had any hope of holding on to her sanity, she couldn't think about Chase anymore tonight. She just couldn't.

The orders for her specialized lingerie were coming in faster than she could fill them. It seemed she had fewer hours in each day, especially since her father-in-law's recent stroke. Due to his poor health, the responsibility for the bulk of the Alexander business holdings had fallen onto her shoulders.

In a moment of self-pity, Josie wondered if there would ever come a time when she wouldn't have to put her own hopes and dreams on hold in order to please someone else.

Now on top of everything else, there was Chase Fowler to deal with.

Alone, with no one to witness the weakness, Josie tunneled her fingers through her hair, bent her head over the silent, momentarily unproductive sewing machine, and gave in to the anguished tears she'd held back for so long.

CHASE'S FOOT pressed harder on the accelerator and his grip tightened on the steering wheel. Wind rushed through the open window of the truck, carrying the scent of alfalfa.

His was the only truck on the open country road. Normally he didn't mind being alone, but tonight was different.

Fields stretched for miles on either side of him. He had an urge to get in his plane and defy the laws of nature. Flying a foot off the ground at 120 knots created an adrenaline surge comparable only to good sex. But a half-million-dollar airplane wasn't a good place to be when a man had heavy things on his mind.

Dodging trees and high wires, or even something as simple as a neglected shovel left standing between the rows of bushy cotton required absolute concentration. With the surprises and turmoil he'd experienced today, he'd have to have a death wish to climb into the cockpit of his air tractor tonight.

God Almighty, he was a father.

He didn't know how he'd managed to have a fairly rational discussion with Josie on the subject without it turning into an all-out war. He didn't know how he'd managed to hold his emotions in hand. But he knew that the innocent person in all this was a little boy. From bitter experience Chase knew what it was like to have your life pulled apart by the stigma of illegitimacy. By pushing the issue, he could very well inflict the same wounds on his own son that he himself had suffered as a child. Still, his own moral code and sense of responsibility begged to be satisfied.

Admittedly, he hadn't given a lot of thought to fatherhood. He'd been too busy making plans, building up his crop-dusting business. Now, in less than a day, just eight short hours, his world had been rocked right down to its foundation.

He had a son.

With the stars bright overhead and the smell of hay soothing his turmoil, Chase made a decision to change his tactics. He'd promised himself four years ago that if he ever found this woman again, he'd hold on to her, learn her secrets, woo her, erase the soul-deep sadness that had mesmerized him so, haunted him for four long years.

The one secret he hadn't counted on uncovering—that they'd made a baby together—suddenly tilted his world. It also upped the stakes of his plans.

Because Chase had an agenda that was as personal and important to him as his name. He wasn't quite sure how it'd come out, or when, but he had some surprises of his own that could very well rock this small Louisiana town.

And Josie Alexander, it seemed, was caught smack in the middle.

THE ROOSTER started crowing before dawn. Josie was sure that the darn bird had gone senile. In all the years she'd had him, he'd never once timed his morning call right.

Her eyes felt as if they were coated with sand, but trying for an extra hour of sleep was futile.

That was Chase Fowler's fault, she thought sourly. Her traitorous mind had conjured up illicit, erotic dreams of second-rate motel rooms and a dark, sexy stranger. As much as she'd fought them, the night pictures would not cease. They left her hot and edgy and aching for something she had no business even thinking about.

Sighing, Josie threw her legs over the side of the bed and drew on an old pair of jeans and sneakers. The rooster gave another piercing, five-note call. She hoped the stillness of predawn would carry the racket across the cotton field, right into Chase Fowler's ears. Misery loves company and all that, she thought.

After she'd fed the chickens and gathered the eggs, Josie showered and dressed in a denim skirt and ivory shell. The humidity was already making her skin crawl and it wasn't even eight o'clock yet.

Having loaded the Bronco and cleaned up the house, she strapped J.T. into his car seat and headed into town. The boy chattered the whole way, exclaiming over each cow and stray dog they passed, as if he'd never seen one in his life. Josie tried to keep him occupied, but it was getting increasingly difficult with each mile they traveled. She felt cranky and, well...conspicuous—as if everyone in town had somehow learned her secret.

Rationally, she knew that wasn't the case. Chase Fowler might have been angry and determined, but he had a gentle streak, a southern code of honor that would prevent him from destroying her life on a whim. She certainly didn't know him well enough to be making such a character judgment, but she believed it deep down in her soul.

Foolish woman, she thought. It wouldn't do to let her guard down. Show your vulnerabilities and people had a tendency to walk over you without a backward glance. A person wouldn't dream of stepping on a rose, but they'd tread on a dandelion and never even consider the slight destruction.

"Play with the kids, Mama?"

Josie glanced over at J.T. who had his little hands resting on the padded safety bar of the car seat. "Yes, darling. As soon as we see Aunt Dottie, I'll take you over to Mary Alice's."

"'kay."

Josie smiled. She knew that J.T. looked forward to the two days a week he spent at the day-care center. Mary Alice Temple ran the center out of a little building her husband had built for her on their property. She was a natural with children and truly one of the sweetest people Josie had ever known.

She and Josie had been best friends since grade school. They'd cried over pimples and boys and griped about curfews, which they'd sworn were ruining their lives forever. They'd whispered about sex, gossiped worse than the old ladies down at the garden club, and made outlandish, yet oh-so-solemn predictions about who'd be the first to get their period or their boobs. They'd competed as only true friends can compete, yet always remained strong and fierce in their loyalty to each other. There'd never been a single secret between them.

Except one.

Josie glanced over at J.T. as she parked the Bronco in front of a small dress shop on Main Street. Every time she looked at his sweet face, she felt incredible joy. She was so blessed. Her chest tightened and she had to make a conscious effort to relax. There was no way she'd allow her own sin to touch this baby's life. Right now, that seemed like an impossible vow to keep, but Josie wouldn't let that stop her. She'd think of something.

"Hey, Aunt Dottie." Trying to keep a firm grip on the padded hangers in her hand, Josie set J.T. down next to a rack of women's blouses and threaded her way through the small dress shop toward the tiny woman behind the counter. The place smelled of lilacs and peppermints, scents that had been Dottie Alexander's trademark for as long as Josie could remember. Her great-aunt by marriage—Bobby's great-aunt—Josie felt closer to this woman than even her own mother.

"Hey, hon. You look tired."

Josie smiled and bent down to kiss Dottie's cheek, careful not to smudge the rouge and caked powder. Josie admired Aunt Dottie's soft, young-looking skin, to which the older woman strongly credited her years of dedication to Ponds cold cream. "I'm a little beat. I stayed up late to finish this order."

"Well, let me just get a look at these newest creations."

Josie displayed the items she'd brought: a silk chemise in rich turquoise, boxer-style pajamas fashioned out of brocade satin, a whispery-soft camisole and tap pants in crepe de chine, and a dramatic electric blue teddy, alluringly sheer and silky with a dyed-to-match Venice lace insert to create an illusion of modesty.

"My land, these are wicked." Dottie chuckled and hung the lingerie on a special rack.

All of Josie's designs were wickedly sensual, to the absolute delight of her customers. Even women who worked their farms alongside their husbands appreciated the incredibly feminine, sensuous slide of silk against their bodies. Josie had taken that into account when she'd designed her first piece of lingerie. The major part of her clientele might wear practical jeans and shirts and boots, but beneath those work clothes their bodies were encased in pure sin.

Dottie shook her head and with a twinkle in her crystal blue eyes, said, "Rumor has it that husbands around these parts are having trouble concentrating on farm equipment. Some folks are blamin' that on you, Josie Mae."

"Have I started a scandal, Aunt Dottie?" She'd meant the words in fun, but her conscience didn't quite get the message. Guilt swamped her, making her feel as if her secret were flashing like a neon sign across her forehead. Instinctively, she looked around for J.T., who had his nose pressed against the glass display case.

"A shrewd business scandal, the best kind." Aunt Dottie didn't seem to pick up on anything being amiss. "My lady friends down at the garden club claim you're partly responsible for the growing population in northeast Louisiana."

Josie laughed. "Aunt Dottie, you're teasing me." She looked around again for her son. "Oh, no. J.T., honey, don't lick the glass. You know how Aunt Dottie hates to clean it."

"Leave that child be. A few fingerprints and slobber never hurt nobody. Besides, I keep telling you I'm about ready to retire. If you take over the shop like you've always wanted, that baby's fingerprints on the case there will come to be your trademark."

"No, it just means I'll be the one cleaning it all the time. And I'd much rather have my lingerie be my trademark."

"No doubt about that, child. Given the right environment and approach, you could stand to make a mint."

Josie sighed. That was a dream she tried not to covet too fiercely. "Someday, Aunt Dottie. Don't give up on me."

"Leroy putting more pressure on you?"

"I don't mind."

"Don't be so cotton pickin' agreeable. I might be an old lady, but my eyesight is just fine. Since Bobby's gone, you been wearing yourself out trying to pick up the slack. Let Harold earn his keep for a while. It's what Leroy pays him for, isn't it?''

"The land was Bobby's pride and joy, Aunt Dottie. You know that. And besides, Harold's not family."

"Sound's just like something Leroy would say. You tell that nephew of mine to turn loose of some of his cash and get you some help. You got a life to live, girl. See to your dreams now, while you're young."

If only there was an abundance of cash to turn loose of, Josie thought. It was for that reason that she'd had to sell off the adjacent land to Chase. And wasn't that just a kick in the pants? The true financial position of the Alexanders was a well-guarded secret, and Josie was one of a very few who was privy to that information. Talk about trademarks, wanted or otherwise. It seemed she'd become the queen of secrets lately.

"Soon, Aunt Dottie." Josie bent down and kissed her aunt's cheek. "Thanks for caring." She held out her hand for J.T. "Ready to go, sweetie?"

"In your spare time," Dottie said with a devilish smirk that portrayed pure fun and a wealth of love, "see what you can do about designing me one of them fancy brassieres. I've a mind to shake up a couple of old fuddy-duddy's over at the garden club. Who knows. Might even start a new fad."

"Aunt Dottie," Josie said, feigning shock, "I'm surprised at you."

"Oh, go on with you now. Ain't nowhere it says that young folks can have all the fun."

"You're absolutely right. But give me some guidelines here. Are we talking soft and sexy, or hard-core Madonna?"

Dottie pretended to consider, which didn't fool Josie for a minute. "Soft and sexy I'd imagine... and scandalous."

Josie grinned. "I've got the perfect idea. You'll love it." Pausing, with the front door open, she looked back over her shoulder. "And so will Mr. Potts."

After she'd dropped J.T. off at Mary Alice's, Josie drove on over to the Alexanders'. Unlike her own house, this one was showy, set alone on top of a hill. For as long as she'd known him, Leroy had joked that he liked being high up so he could look out on his town to keep an eye on things.

Two stories, the huge house was painted white with thick round columns along the front. Flowers bloomed everywhere in a profusion of color, tended by a gardener. Inez Alexander, Josie's mother-in-law, had never known a day's work in the beautiful gardens, except when she donned her straw hat and gloves and cut flowers to take indoors for the help to arrange in vases.

In addition to the gardener, Inez and Leroy employed a cook and a maid. There were always wonderful smells coming out of the kitchen. Through the back entrance on the service porch, the heat of recent ironing made the swirling fans almost obsolete. The clean smell of starch and bleach was as much a part of this room as the walls themselves.

As a young girl, Josie had spent a lot of time in the kitchen and service porch of this stately old house. She'd been the daughter of the Alexanders' seamstress. Keeping with proper etiquette, it had been subtly suggested by Inez that Josie use the back entrance like the rest of the help.

Though her marriage to Bobby afforded her the right to use the front door now, Josie resisted. She wasn't in the mood to suffer censured looks should she happen to run into Inez.

Winding her way from the back of the house, she found Leroy in the front room sitting in his wheelchair, gazing out the window. His pale blue eyes brightened, an expression he instantly tried to cover. But Josie had his number. He might appear to be a gruff old man, but he was a marshmallow inside.

She bent down to kiss him. "Reporting for duty, sir."

"'Bout time you got here. Cheeky little thing, ain't ya." His speech was slow, but fairly clear. The stroke had left him without the full use of his right arm and leg. One of his eyes and the side of his mouth drooped slightly. It hurt Josie to see the once vibrant man in this condition, but she never let on.

"Five-eight is not little, Leroy."

"Suppose not. Where's that grandson of mine?"

Josie's heart did a weird little tumble, but she didn't miss a beat. "J.T.'s over at Mary Alice's."

Leroy harumphed. He didn't cotton to kids going to fancy day-care centers. It was a good-natured argument they'd had many times.

"How's that ol' boy up by you makin' out with the new airstrip?"

Again, her heart lurched. "Fine, I guess." She hadn't expected this line of conversation. It made her uncomfortable. She hoped to heaven Leroy wouldn't notice. Since Josie had handled the sale of the land,

and met the new owner, Leroy had no way of knowing that Chase wasn't an *old* boy.

"Best see to gettin' them fields sprayed before the varmints eat up the whole shootin' match."

Before Josie could voice an objection, Leroy started ticking off a list of things that needed to be done.

"Just make yourself at home in the library. Files are all set up and the phone numbers are in the book there. It's gettin' on about the first of the month and them lease payments are due. You be sure and keep an eye on the managers. Them sapsuckers'll drag their feet if they figure they can get away with it."

"Yes, sir."

Leroy looked at Josie for a long minute as if just now realizing how much responsibility he was dropping on her shoulders. "It's times like this I miss my boy."

She laid a hand on his shoulder and squeezed. "I miss him too, Leroy."

As if that little bit of melancholy was not to be tolerated, Leroy jutted out his chin. "You're like a daughter to me, Missy. You got a right good head on your neck, there. Ain't no doubt in my mind you can handle this business stuff."

"Thank you. I'll do my best."

"Humph. You'll do better than that, girly. Always have," he said by way of a compliment. "Can't let folks think I'm not watchin' out for what's mine. You'll have to be my eyes and legs since the ones I've got have decided to go useless on me. After all, this'll be J.T.'s some day. Gotta keep things up to snuff."

Josie was starting to feel overwhelmed. "Leroy, you have more faith in me than I do myself sometimes."

"Oh, go on with you. That son of mine knew what he was doin' when he picked you."

"Contrary to popular opinion?"

One of Leroy's brows pulled inward in an attempt to frown. "Whose?"

"Miz Alexander doesn't share your sentiments."

Leroy dismissed that with an impatient, sluggish lift of his left hand. "Inez can be uppity sometimes. Southern ladies and all that. But you've got more on the ball than flitting to every charity in town and having servants to do your work for you. Like I said, Bobby knew what he was about."

In a spontaneous gesture that usually embarrassed her father-in-law, Josie leaned down and gave him a hug.

"About the crops," Josie said, feeling as if she had a yellow streak running right down the center of her back. "I'm not sure about—"

"Get Harold on it. He's got maps showing the layout of our land. Knows what chemicals to use and where. Stuff's already been ordered and setting in the barn out yonder." He lifted his hand in a vague gesture of direction. "Have him haul it over to the dusters. They'll take care of it from there."

Josie let out a sigh of relief. She was more than glad to turn that portion of the operation over to Harold. She'd just as soon avoid Chase Fowler if at all possible.

An hour later, sitting at the massive cherry wood desk, she'd dealt with the backlog of paperwork and phone calls. Harold was the last call on her list and it was with a sinking heart that she listened to his distracted, agitated news. It seemed his son over in Arkansas had tangled with an eight-ton tractor. The outcome didn't look good and Harold was headed out just as soon as he could get his wife in the truck and his kids farmed out to the neighbors.

Responding to the distress in his voice, Josie urged him to get going and assured him she'd collect his kids from school and make sure they got settled in at the Henderson place. With a sigh, she hung up the phone and rubbed at her temple, which had begun to feel as if an angry woodpecker had been turned loose inside her head.

The last place she wanted to go was the airport.

HEAT WAVES SHIMMERED like a mirage, hovering over the asphalt and rippling like invisible flags off the hood of the pickup. Added to the crushing heat, the smell of chemicals fairly blasted through the open window of the truck, a residual odor from the spray booms of the crop dusters.

Her headache intensified.

Josie shut off the engine and got out of the truck. The sign over the hangar said Fowler's Flying Service. Even without it, she'd have known she was in the right place. Planes were everywhere for one thing, and she was very nearly within shouting distance of her own home.

The term next-door neighbor—or being neighborly—was starting to take on a new meaning.

Especially in view of who that neighbor was.

Her heart lurched when she caught sight of a man heading her way, then settled down to normal when she recognized who it was. Lord above, if she didn't calm down she'd be courting an early grave.

"Hey, Junior." Junior Watkins came from a family of eight. Josie had gone to school with his older sister, Katie. It seemed she'd gone to school with just about everyone in these parts. Everyone except Chase. "How's the family? And Katie?"

"Family's good. Katie's over in Dallas now. Married and got three youngun's. She'd like to hear from you."

"I know. I ought to write. So what's happening with you?"

Junior grinned. "Holly's expecting. I'm gonna be a daddy come Christmastime."

"Well, hey, congratulations." Junior and Holly had only been married a month. The gossips down at Sunny's Diner were going to have a heyday counting on their fingers. Which, of course, wouldn't hold a candle to what would happen if they got wind of *her* secret.

"You lookin' for Chase?"

"Yes." At the mere mention of his name, butterflies took flight in her stomach.

Junior grinned again, this time with a sheepish hint of awe. "I got me a job flying these babies." He gestured toward the row of yellow planes parked at an angle outside the hangar. "Boss's in the office over there. Want me to unload your pickup?"

Josie laughed and lifted her hands in a shrugging indication that she was a little out of her depth. "I suppose. You'd probably know better than me." Too bad she couldn't get Junior to handle the spraying, too. That way she'd never have to even see Chase Fowler at all.

CHASE WATCHED HER through the office window. Seeing her get out of the truck caused his stomach to feel as if he'd just hit an air pocket at ten thousand feet. Watching her full lips widen in laughter made his loins tighten and his jealousy flair.

She'd never laughed like that for him. In the three times they'd encountered one another, her expressive green eyes had shown either desperation, passion, shock or aggression. The only tenderness or light moments he'd witnessed were the times when she looked at her son. *His* son.

He found himself wanting to be the one responsible for making her laugh, for lightening the heavy load she seemed to carry on her slim shoulders. He wanted the right to help her raise that little boy. Wanted the right to hold her in the night when the weight of the world closed in on her.

Wanted to be the only man in her life with those rights.

And if he didn't stop thinking along these lines he was liable to storm outside and throttle that darn kid he'd just hired.

She came through the door looking classy yet casual in a denim skirt and sleeveless white top. Both garments clung in all the right places and Chase wasn't above staring. Especially at the outline of lace beneath the clingy cotton shell.

Just her presence made his small office seem dingy. The oscillating fan did little more than stir papers off his metal desk, scattering them on the dust-covered concrete floor. It was stifling hot and sticky in here, he realized with a touch of embarrassment. Funny how he hadn't thought of turning on the air conditioner until Josie Alexander entered the room.

He walked over and pushed the button marked High Cool on the wall unit, then dragged a metal chair across the floor and proceeded to beat the dust off the brown seat.

"Sit down." He grinned when she eyed the chair as if it were alive. "Hey, live a little. Besides, it's probably not any worse than that pickup out there."

She lit into that chair with a fair amount of determination and an obvious lift of her chin. His grin widened. Give the lady a challenge and she'd meet it, he mused. He'd have to remember that.

"I suppose white wasn't the wisest choice this morning." She relented and halfway returned his smile. "Then again, this wasn't on my schedule."

"No? I'll admit I'm surprised to see you." Especially with the way they'd parted the night before. He nodded toward the dusty Ford Junior was still unloading. "Got a lot of poison out there."

Her confidence seemed to slip a bit. "I have a map."

Chase started to frown, then caught himself. He leaned a hip against the rickety old desk, careful to keep his other foot firmly on the floor in case the thing decided to collapse. "That's usually a good idea."

She stood and thrust a manila folder at him as if she couldn't wait to have it out of her hands. "Harold's real good about keeping records. Everything is listed in detail. You shouldn't have any trouble figuring out which chemicals go on which crops."

"I take it you're hiring me to do your spraying?"

"Well, yes...I thought..."

Chase's gaze seemed to linger of its own accord on her legs...long, long legs, bare from the above the knee length of her skirt to her polished toenails. She was standing so close to him now, her legs nearly brushing against his. Sunlight somehow found its way through the dirty windowpanes, glancing off her silky brown hair, making it shine with golden highlights. Her scent was natural, fresh, erotic in its simplicity.

Suddenly, Chase became aware of the silence. Her words had stopped midflow. Their eyes met and neither seemed able to look away. Time stood frozen in that instant. All around them were sounds: the whine of a turbine engine, shouts from a pilot, the bang of metal clanging against chain as a roll-up door was lowered or raised, an airplane overhead, circling. But those sounds were in another dimension. He noticed nothing except the woman before him, the smoothness of her skin, her femininity, the incredible magnetism that arced between them like a furious electrical storm.

Slowly, as if drawn by a magnet, his gaze slipped lower, to her full lips, wet and slick, their color an exact match of her nail polish. He knew how those lips would fit against his, had dreamed about it—relived it—for years. The image of her lipstick smudging, sliding against his lips like slick, scented oil made his body grow even harder.

It took all of his control to pull back from her. Once before he'd given in to the incredible pull of this woman—and she'd left him without a backward glance. The next time he had her in that particular, sensual position, he intended to make damn sure it was his name that hovered against her lips. Next time—and there would be a next time—he wouldn't make it easy for her to walk away.

Chase forced his thoughts back to the business at hand. "I studied entomology," he managed to say with a fair amount of composure.

"What?" The hitch in her voice nearly crumbled his good intentions.

"The chemicals. I'm darn good when it comes to pests and crop diseases."

"Oh."

"Which means I'll get it right the first time."

All at once she seemed to realize how close they were standing and she backed up, tugging her skirt when, in his opinion, it didn't need tugging at all.

"Good. Then should I sign something? A contract?"

"This isn't your normal thing, is it?"

"No. I don't know all the ins and outs of farming—just what Bobby taught me. But I'm learning. I've never had to deal with this particular end of the business before."

He admired the fact that she'd admit it. Most people would at least try to bluff. But Josie was not most people, as he'd found out when he'd gone over to Sunny's Diner for breakfast. Hell, in small towns, folks just loved to talk about other folks.

She was a people pleaser, Jake down at the Feed and Seed had said. *Took care of that husband of hers, never leavin' his side. Takes care of old Leroy now. Never hear no complainin' out of that little gal. Active in the church and community and'll do anything for ya. Been stepped on a time or two by wellmeanin' folks, probably 'cause she's so goodhearted. Never hear an unkind word come out of her mouth. No siree. 'Cept maybe if you was to talk bad about one of her own. She'll stand up to anyone right*

*quick if you was to go and do that. Smart as a whip
and talented. . . .*

Jake had gone on, but Chase didn't need convinc-
ing. He'd already made up his mind that this was a
lady worth getting to know better. The fact that she
was the mother of his child presented a complication, especially in view of her resistance. But it was
a complication he felt sure they could come to terms
on.

"How come you're handling the chemicals?
Where's the big man?"

"The big man?" She frowned. "Do you mean
Leroy?"

"He's the one who seems to own most of these
parts."

She seemed to hesitate for just a moment. "Yes. I
suppose he does."

"Then why isn't he out here taking care of business?"

"Leroy's had some health problems."

Chase felt an odd tightening in his chest, but he
deliberately kept his tone casual. "What's wrong
with him?"

"He had a stroke."

There it was again—that odd little punch. "And
you're handling the farm?"

"Yes." Josie's chin jutted out. "As well as nego-
tiating leases, collecting rent, hiring mechanics for
the farm equipment and trying to get an updated irrigation system off the ground."

And raising my son, he thought. "That's a lot for
one person to handle. What's in it for you?"

"It's family."

"Your late husband's family."

"My son's family. The Alexander legacy is his."
Josie could have bitten her tongue. Of all the things
to say, especially to this particular man. She was
flustered and needed to get herself under control.
Although she fought it, the incredible pull of attraction between them was about to get the better of her.

His raised brow seemed to mock her, causing a
nagging sense of guilt to rear its head. Was J.T. really the rightful heir to the Alexander heritage? Bi-
ologically speaking, only she knew the truth.

But that wasn't the case anymore, she reminded
herself. Chase Fowler also knew the truth.

"Leroy has always taken care of the folks here in
this town . . . and me. He's having a rough time right
now. He thinks of me like a daughter and I appreciate that. So until he's back on his feet, I'm more than
glad to help him out, to try and give back just a small
measure of what he's given."

"You make the guy sound like some kind of saint.
From what I've heard about Leroy Alexander, seems
to me you might be looking at him with blinders on."

"My father-in-law is a good man." Josie's de-
fenses rose. Chase's tone had a tight quality that she
couldn't quite decipher.

"Good men don't refuse to recognize their illegitimate kids."

"What are you talking about?" This didn't make
any sense. Up until now Chase had all but demanded that he be able to openly recognize J.T. How
had they switched subjects so quickly?

"I'm talking about my father."

"Your father?" She felt like a parrot, but for the
life of her she couldn't keep up with this conversation.

"My birth father," he said. "The man who refused to recognize me and my mother. The man who left us dirt poor when he could have done something about it." He paused, his jaw tight, his dark eyes fierce. "The man whose name is Leroy Alexander."

A split second of silence rang out as the name echoed off the walls of the dingy office. Josie's knees nearly buckled.

Oh, dear God in Heaven, it couldn't be. Surely she hadn't slept with Bobby's *brother!*

Chapter Four

Josie shook her head wildly. "I don't believe you!"

"My mother wasn't a liar, Josie," he said tightly. "And I use the term father very loosely. I'm talking strictly biological, here."

"Biologic—but . . ." No, it couldn't be. His tone was defensive, terse, with an underlying thread of pain. She refused to recognize that hurt, or the validity of his claim. "Leroy would have said something," she challenged. "*Bobby* would have said something. This has got to be some sort of a trick."

His eyes narrowed, causing her to back up a step. "Remember this?" He pointed to his shoulder.

"What?"

"The birthmark."

"What of it?"

"My great-grandfather—James Troy—had it, too."

Josie felt perspiration drip down her palms. She couldn't think straight. Oh, God, she had to think. Was there a trap here? Her hands trembled as she shoved them through her hair.

J.T. had been named after Bobby's great-grandfather—at Leroy's prompting. In view of the banana-shaped mark on the baby's tiny shoulder, it had seemed fitting...and an absolute answer to prayers. She'd even wondered, if by some miracle... But no, that was ludicrous. She'd decided that Leroy was just caught up in the emotion of the birth of his grandson, that he'd seen in a simple mark of nature exactly what he'd *wanted* to see.

And now, before her, stood Chase Fowler, clearing up a three-year mystery she'd all but dismissed—and throwing her life into utter chaos in the process.

"Does anybody else know about this?" Surely not. The gossip mill would have nearly torched itself with the speed of spreading the word.

"I'm not exactly in Leroy's confidence. Based on thirty-two years of silence, I'd venture to say you'd know better than me."

"My God, I slept with my husband's brother." The words were out before she could stop them. Josie sank into the vinyl chair, overwhelmed. She'd thought things were bad before, now they'd turned into a hellish mess.

He didn't say anything for several seconds, just stood there, rigid, watching her, his hands jammed into the front pockets of his jeans. Then he quirked one eyebrow. "I wonder if you're really that good an actress."

"Now what are you implying?"

"I'm not quite sure. Like I said before, you don't fit the mold of a one night stand. But I can't help but wonder if you didn't get pregnant just to hang on to the Alexander money."

"That's ridiculous. I was married to Bobby Alexander."

"My half brother," he reminded her. "Who was terminally ill."

Josie just stared at him. Something inside her felt on the verge of exploding. She wrapped her arms around her middle as if she could hold the madness at bay. He was dead wrong about her reasons. Money had never been an issue. *Love.* That's why she'd done it. Only for love.

"Maybe you went through my wallet that night four years ago."

"I did no such thing." She was actually affronted that he'd even suggest the devious behavior.

"You had the opportunity. I was asleep. One minute you were in my arms, all soft and sexy and sated. The next thing I remember I woke up and you'd vanished without a trace. I had no idea who you were, but I have to wonder if you weren't fully aware of who *I* was."

"Chase, that's absurd. And why would I even connect the name Fowler with Alexander? I'd picked you up on the side of the road, for God's sake. You were just a face, a body." Her memories of that night came flooding back, swamping her, overwhelming her with their power.

The fine thread of rationality she'd been holding on to snapped, releasing the madness. She couldn't stop the words that tumbled out, words she'd never said to another living soul.

"Bobby wanted a baby so badly. We'd been trying. I knew I was ovulating. But the doctor had just given me some devastating news about Bobby's true condition—he wouldn't be able to father children. The medication they were experimenting with, it had done something to his body. I thought, God, if only

I was already pregnant. My body was willing, it was the perfect time...it would have been the perfect gift.

"Bobby deserved to have his heart's desire. He was a fabulous man. The best. I would have done anything for him." She didn't realize that tears were tracking down her cheeks until a splash of warmth fell onto her clenched hands.

"And you did." Chase's quiet voice broke through the shroud of her past. She felt the gentle touch of his palm against the side of her face as he encouraged her to look at him. She hadn't been aware that he'd moved, hadn't even noticed when he'd squatted down in front of her. This behavior switch, coming on the heels of his nastiness just moments before, had her thoroughly off-balance.

"Did what?" she whispered.

"You gave Bobby his dream. My brother was a lucky guy." Chase shook his head. Josie and Bobby, and most especially J.T., were technically the innocents here. He shouldn't be fighting with her over his beef with Leroy. The main issue he wanted to take up with Josie had to do with his son.

"Seems to me you've spent a fair amount of time taking care of everybody else. Who takes care of you, sugar?"

He saw her green eyes fill first with protest, then gratitude. Hadn't anyone ever told this woman how special she was? Once again Chase found himself wanting to ease her burdens.

"I can handle your farming needs. That's my job. But I'd like to do more. Be more. Let me take care of you for a while...you and my son."

"No."

"Don't do this to me, Josie. I'm not pushing you to acknowledge my paternity to the town." He didn't realize how much it would bother him to say that. But he had little choice in the matter. The woman before him was on the verge of breaking. He could see the fragile thread she held on to like a lifeline. Still, he had to try to make her understand his needs.

"Because of the circumstances of my own birth, I need to take some responsibility. I *want* to. I want to know my son."

Josie felt everything within her become utterly still. She searched his vivid eyes, eyes that could gleam with suppressed amusement, or sharpen with intelligence, or cut like blue lasers in anger. She'd witnessed each of these emotions at one time or another. Right now, though, she caught a fleeting glimpse of hope. A silent plea. It had come and gone so quickly that she might have missed it if she hadn't been looking so closely.

But she *had* been looking. And darn it all, that suppressed emotion had gotten a hold of her. She knew it wouldn't let go.

"All right. You have a right to get to know J.T. But as far as taking care of me—of us," she amended. "that's out."

"Why?"

"It just is." She knew he was about to argue. "Don't push me on this, Chase."

JOSIE WAS TENDING the vegetable garden when she heard Chase's truck come up the driveway. "Dang it." She snatched out another weed, then stood, wiping her dirty hands on the seat of her denim shorts. Either the days were getting shorter or time was speeding up. She was nowhere near getting the chores done, and now she'd have to stop and entertain company.

The thought of just who that company was caused her heart to trip. Why had she ever agreed to this arrangement?

J.T., who'd been sitting smack in the middle of the cucumbers and lettuce, popped up. "Dang it," he parroted.

Josie started to admonish him, then realized that to do so would only call attention to the slang words, making them new and curious. In that case, J.T. would surely test them out again. Best just to watch her own language, she decided.

J.T. raced around the corner of the house, then abruptly veered off course as a startled robin flew out from beneath an azalea bush. "Oh! Dat birdie scared me!"

Chase was close enough to have witnessed the little boy jump. Grinning, he squatted down so that he was eye level with J.T. "Naw. You probably scared him worse."

J.T. seemed to like this idea. "Hi, man. What's dat?"

"J.T.!" The tone of her voice had her son glancing over his shoulder, the stubborn frown on his face clearly stating he didn't see anything wrong with his inquiry. Chase, too, glanced up. She'd never understood what it meant to be held by a man's eyes. Now she knew.

Dragging her gaze away, she frowned down at her son. "The man's name is Mr. Fowler—"

"Chase," he corrected softly.

"I 'member," J.T. chimed in. "Whatja got?"

Josie let out a weary sigh and shook her head. It looked as if her lesson in manners would not be met with either comprehension or cooperation.

Chase held up the object in his hand. "It's for you. An airplane, sort of like the one I fly."

"Oh, boy!" J.T. started to reach for it, then remembered himself and looked back at Josie. "'Kay, Mama?"

She nodded absently, unable to take her eyes off the gentle, reverent, awed expression on Chase's face as he looked at his son. J.T. cradled the toy plane in his small hands, then took off at a run, his sound effects several octaves off-key.

"J.T." Josie called. "What do you say?"

"Thank you, Mr. Chase."

"Just Chase," he corrected.

"'Kay."

Josie's gaze riveted on the flex of muscles in Chase's thighs as he rose. His attention was still on J.T., who frolicked in grass that hadn't seen the blade of a tractor in way too long. Her heartbeat thudded in what she was coming to recognize as fear. She'd agreed that he should know his son, but she suddenly wanted to take back the words.

He was a fine specimen of a man, but she couldn't stop thinking about Chase being Bobby's half brother. Now that she was looking for it, she supposed there were similarities. He had the Alexander coloring, and their heights were a pretty good match—Bobby had been tall and slender. But that's about where the comparison ended.

There was something extra about Chase, a certain look or attitude that could generate both fear and respect. He had the look of a bad boy about him, with his midnight hair swept straight back off his forehead and a slight five o'clock shadow covering his upper lip and chin. His blue eyes were serious now as he watched J.T. play in the yard, but Josie had seen the corners of those eyes crinkle in amusement or the dimples in his cheeks flash in moments of teasing . . . or passion.

There was no doubt about it, this was the type of guy that had daddies wanting to lock away their daughters. *Lean* and *tough* were the words that came to mind when she looked at Chase . . . and sexy.

Lordy, Lordy. A wave of guilt nearly buckled her knees. Here she stood, in the side yard of the house she and Bobby had lived in, admitting to herself that she was passionately attracted to another man . . . Bobby's *brother*.

"You okay, sugar?"

That lazy drawl of his was going to be her undoing. "You shouldn't be buying my son gifts." She was appalled at her snappy tone.

His distinctive blue eyes gleamed with amusement as he held his hands up in a gesture of surrender. "It's just a toy. There's no call to get violent over it."

Josie hadn't realized she was holding the gardening spade in front of her like a weapon. She felt a little foolish. In spite of herself, she returned his grin. "Sorry."

"Okay, tiger. Lead me to the bed."

"I beg your pardon?"

"Now where in the world, I wonder, is your mind?" His grin widened as he advanced on her in that slow moving, dangerously sexy way that had her heart and stomach changing places. "Did you forget why I was here?"

Surely she hadn't given him the impression that...

"The crib?" he reminded. "The bed that needs hauling down from the attic?"

Josie had the good sense to step out of his reach before he could touch her. This man's touch could send her up in flames. Knowing that, admitting it, upset her to no end. He was dangerous. He had the ammunition to unravel the whole fabric of her life. And her son's.

She couldn't allow herself to forget that. Couldn't allow herself to be swept away by his charm, by the vivid, erotic memories of his touch. No matter how much she yearned to relive that touch, she just couldn't.

"This way." She stalked around him and nearly broke into a run in her rush to get to the house.

"Uh, Josie?"

"What?" She'd just reached the front screen door and was in the process of pulling it open when his voice stopped her. It sounded suspiciously as if he were about to strangle on laughter.

"You've got dirt on you."

"Where?"

"Your butt." Straight faced, he brushed by her and let himself in the house in a slow moving, yet purposeful stride. "Nice butt, too."

Josie whipped around and brushed at her backside. "Charming of you to point that out for me," she muttered.

His chuckle told her he'd heard her.

"You might as well wait up, Chase. You're going to need help getting that bed out of the attic." Turning, she searched for her son. "J.T., honey. You need to come in the house. Mama's got to do something."

"No!"

"Don't tell me no, young man."

"Plane, Mama," he whined.

"I know, sweetie. Bring the plane inside and play for a while."

"Big plane."

"Yes," Josie agreed, distracted. "Inside now."

HE FELT HIS EYES getting a little sleepy, but if he said anything, Mama might make him have supper and go on to bed. He didn't want to do that. Especially since he had this new airplane. The nice man had said it was just like the one he flew. J.T. thought that was pretty neat.

In an effort to keep himself awake, he made several running passes around the living room, trying out different types of airplane sounds. Then he remembered something.

Squirming up on the couch, careful not to drop his toy, J.T. pressed his face against the window. He could see some yellow planes way far past the cotton. When those planes flew over the barn, they looked pretty big. From his place at the window, though . . . J.T. glanced down at the toy in his hand. Why, it looked about the same size to him. Maybe he'd just go on over there and see. If he ran real fast, he could play a little bit, then come back before Mama and Chase got the bed set up. Maybe he could even bring one of those planes back—then he'd have two. He didn't think the big man would mind.

Hopping off the couch, he stuck his fingers in the little crack of the door. He had to set his airplane down and use both hands to pull. When the door popped open, he picked up his toy and skipped real quicklike down the porch steps.

"GOOD GRIEF, I'm hotter than a fox."

Chase cocked an eyebrow and grinned. "I told you I could manage on my own."

"I'm sure you could." Josie's eyes strayed once more to the flex of muscles in his arms. Soon, now, she was going to stop noticing this man's virility. "But Mattie—she's the maid over at the Alexanders who practically raised me—always said that many hands make light work. Now the bed's all put together and the sun's still up."

"We were racing against the sun?"

"Not really. It's just the more daylight hours there are, the more things that can be done."

"In other words, you're busy this evening and you'd like me to be on my way?"

Josie felt her skin heat and hoped he'd put it down to exertion. Why did she suddenly feel tongue-tied? She supposed that all this closeness, watching him strain as he hefted a mattress over his shoulder, or brushing up against him in the tight confines of the attic, was getting to her. Just the sight of him wielding a screwdriver, his long, tapered fingers wrapped around the plastic handle, could send her into an orbit of fantasies.

It was ridiculous. She wasn't normally prone to impulsiveness. Just because she remembered the skill with which this man made love was no reason to let down her guard.

And standing in a room, separated only by the width of a *bed,* was not the place for Josie to be with Chase Fowler.

"I do have some things to do, but..." She hesitated, unsure of what she was about to propose. "If you want, you could play with J.T."

"Kind of like baby-sit?"

"Oh, no. I'll be here—"

"I know what you mean, sugar. I'd like to spend a little time with him. Thank you," he said with quiet sincerity.

She didn't see how she could resist that sincerity. The mother in her was proud of her son, wanted to show him off, wanted everyone in the world to know and see the specialness she saw in her little boy. But inviting—allowing—Chase to be alone with J.T. was courting danger. She wanted to go back on the agreement, yet she couldn't bring herself to do so.

God help her, a selfish part of her actually yearned for his presence, for his steady strength, for the sweet, sensual promise she saw in his eyes. For the reprieve an extra pair of hands would give her. Time to herself. Time to catch up on her lingerie orders which had gotten terribly behind schedule when she'd had to take over Leroy's duties.

Never before had a decision been so fraught with peril. Not even when she'd picked this man up on the highway. Then, she'd acted out of desperation, on impulse. Now she had entirely too much time to think, to worry over every little thing that could go wrong, to anticipate the changes, the risk.

She made the mistake of looking into his eyes. And found herself trapped. Snared like a frightened doe in the high beams of a semi. Afraid to move.

Afraid not to. Even when he came around the bed, she held still, wanting, aching, desire so fierce and powerful she thought she'd scream with her frustration.

Her world became narrowed at that moment, just the two of them. Alone. No obligations, no responsibilities, no outside forces to intrude. She felt his breath against her cheek, saw his pupils dilate, saw his desire and his intent. A man setting his sights on a woman. On her. Her breasts tightened and her heart pounded.

She nearly demanded that he stop the torture, that he kiss her. His thumb swept a path of fire over her lower lip.

"You're not going to change your mind, are you?"

The sound of his voice broke the spell. J.T., she reminded herself. He was asking about J.T.

Josie drew in a swift breath and backed up. What in the world had she been thinking? Her son was in the house, just down the hall, yet she'd forgotten all about him. Chase did that to her. Made her lose all sense of time and place, made her forget just what was at stake between them.

Her stomach was on fire, her legs weak and trembling. It didn't matter what she wanted. Wanting something and allowing herself to have it were two different things.

"No, I'm not going to change my mind," she said at last. She rubbed her damp palms on the seat of her shorts, then wondered if she'd made more hand prints for him to comment on. "I guess you could start by showing J.T. his new furniture. He's being awfully quiet, though. I wonder if he's fallen asleep."

Josie went down the hall and called for J.T. Chase was right behind her. She checked the living room and kitchen, then stopped and frowned. "This isn't like him. He always comes when I call."

"You don't suppose he'd have gone up the attic steps when we had them pulled down, do you?"

"No. At least I don't think so."

"I'd better check and make sure."

Josie was right on his heels as he went back through the hall and pulled the cord that dropped down the ladderlike staircase leading to the attic.

"Stay put," he said. "I'll be right back."

She couldn't have stood still if her life had depended on it. While Chase looked in the attic, Josie checked under the beds, in the closets and the sewing room. When Chase came down shaking his head, she felt rising panic curl through her belly.

At a dead run, she charged back to the front of the house, shouting J.T.'s name. The front door stood ajar. She let out a trembling breath and tried to regain a sense of calm.

"That little stinker. I didn't think he could get this door open. It's warped from the rain, so it sticks." She swallowed hard, aware that her voice sounded breathy, much too bright, aware that she was rambling. "I'm sure I shut it, but it must have stuck on the jamb."

"Are you sure he actually came in earlier?"

"Of course I'm sure." Was that censure she detected in his voice? "What kind of a mother do you think I am?" Oh, God. Her baby was missing. She should never have taken her eyes off him. She'd allowed herself to get caught up in the sensuality of

Chase's eyes, in her own desires, when she should have been thinking about her child.

She didn't wait for Chase's response, for him to validate the terrible guilt she already felt. Instead, she headed off to re-search where she'd already been. Surely she'd just missed him. He was probably curled up someplace next to that old tomcat he loved so much.

But when she'd made a complete circle around the house, her heart clenched in dread. Especially when she saw that Chase, too, was empty-handed.

"Oh, my God. Chase, where can he be? This isn't like him."

"Calm down, Josie. He's probably hiding."

"He wouldn't do that!" Josie ignored his attempt to console her. She ran and searched and ran some more. The locusts were already singing, harmonizing with the tree frogs and crickets. Dusk would not be held at bay. Soon it would be dark. There were no street lights this far out in the country. When darkness fell, it would be final. With no hope of finding a small boy.

Fear nearly crippled her but she couldn't give in. She charged back into the house, screaming J.T.'s name. He wasn't there. She could feel it. Still, she combed every corner of every room. She heard the screen door bang and rushed back through the house.

The genuine worry on Chase's face answered her question before she even asked. "You didn't find him?"

He shook his head.

"Did you check the barn?"

"Yes."

"Oh, God. I should call Bud."

"Who?"

"Bud Temple. Mary Alice's husband. He's the sheriff." She snatched the phone off the hook, but her hands were trembling so badly she dropped it. "I can't remember the number. They'll get a search party. I know they will. The whole town'll come." She grabbed at the dangling cord and upended a drawer in her search for the phone book. "What is that damned number? I should know it by heart!"

Chase caught her by the shoulders and stopped her frantic search. He took the phone from her trembling hands, noticing that his own were none too steady. "Josie, he can only have been gone about fifteen minutes. I've got a cellular phone in the truck. We'll go out and have a look, then if we don't spot him, we'll call in the town."

"But—"

"Trust me, sugar. I've got an idea."

"What?"

"The plane. It'll be faster than waiting for help to arrive clear from town."

His words triggered something in Josie's mind. "Oh, my God, Chase. J.T. was talking about the big planes." She looked out across the cotton field. Sure enough, Chase's yellow crop dusters were visible. "You don't suppose he'd try to make it all the way over there do you?"

Chase looped his arm around Josie's shoulders and brought her up against his chest. For just an instant, he pressed his lips against her temple. It surprised him how easy and right it felt to hold her this way. Comfort offered and accepted between two frightened parents. As it should be. "We'll know in a minute. Come on."

The two-way radio in the truck transmitted to a base unit over in his office as well as the airplanes.

Bubba responded to Chase's call. "Yeah, boss."

"Get the plane up, Bubba. We're looking for a little boy, J.T. Alexander, three years old, he's wearing..." Chase looked at Josie. Her eyes held a look of sheer panic and self-reproach. He knew she'd drawn a blank.

Chase depressed the button on the microphone again. "He's wearing blue shorts and a white T-shirt. Probably carrying a toy airplane. Buzz the cotton and the road between the airstrip and Josie Alexander's place. And Bubba? Get somebody to have a look around the planes."

"Stand by, buddy. I'm airborne in two minutes."

Chase replaced the mike and glanced over at Josie. "We'll find him." He hoped to God he was right. He couldn't bear the thought of losing that little boy. Not when he'd just found him.

"He couldn't have made it all the way over there in this amount of time, could he?"

Chase shrugged. "Kids are amazing sometimes."

"I can't believe I didn't know what he was wearing. What kind of a mother does that make me?"

"A scared one."

"I should have checked on him sooner. If something happens to him, I'll never forgive myself."

It bothered him to see her so torn up. Especially when it reminded him that he was just as vulnerable—and only a breath away from showing it. That would never do.

"Listen up, sugar. That airplane can fly a foot off the ground at 120 knots if need be. In a matter of about five minutes or less, Bubba's gonna have a visual. Then we're going to calmly drive over and pick up our son." That "our son" part got a reaction out of her. Her shoulders squared and her chest puffed out.

"That's the first scenario. The second is, you'll stay here, wringing your hands and heaping guilt on your shoulders and *I'll* calmly go and pick up the boy. Now which is it going to be?"

He was pleased to see that fragile look leave her face. Hell, if the truth be known, he was scared spitless himself.

"Don't you dare talk down to me, Chase Fowler. I'm a mother and I have every right to be upset." She jerked open the passenger door and slid in. Chase got in also, but didn't start the motor.

"What are we waiting for?" Josie demanded. Adrenaline surged in waves of desolate, heartrending terror. She hated the inactivity, the waiting, just *knew* she could outrun any vehicle or airplane, propelled solely on the power of a mother's love.

"For Bubba. No sense taking off on a wild-goose chase. Let's see what Bubba spots from the air. At least it'll give us a direction to start."

Josie was about to object when static crackled out of the radio. Chase didn't give Bubba an opportunity to talk.

He keyed the mike. "Did you find him?"

"That's a roger. Thirty-seven rows of cotton in from where you are. Looks like he was headed our way and got sidetracked. Got an old tomcat under one arm and a toy in the other." Bubba chuckled. "Mighty big load for the little man to carry."

Josie reached over and pulled Chase's hand toward her so she could speak into the mike. "Thank you, Bubba." Her voice trembled with heartfelt emotion.

"Sure thing, ma'am. Just head on up the service road and you'll intercept him. Ya'll better hurry though. He's waving at me and jumpin' up and down. At this rate, he's liable to strangle that poor cat."

"We're on our way." She smiled, then looked at Chase who was sitting stock-still in the driver's seat. His eyes held both relief and a sharpened awareness. Relief because J.T. was his son, too. He'd been as worried as she, Josie realized. Awareness because in her haste to thank Bubba via the microphone, she'd cupped his hand between her own. The position had her lips practically touching his fingers and her breast pressed solidly, erotically against his forearm.

To her everlasting horror, she felt her face flame. As gracefully as possible she released his hand and scooted back to her side of the truck. "We'd better get going."

Chase released a long breath, replaced the mike and put the truck in gear. "It'd be the smart thing to do," he mumbled.

Chapter Five

Darkness surrounded them as they sat on the porch. Josie had a million things to do, but for now she set those thoughts aside. She was content just to hold J.T. in her arms. And if she were to be brutally honest, it felt pretty good having Chase there to share this quiet part of the evening.

"I'm sorry I fell apart awhile ago."

"It's understandable."

"You probably think I'm a terrible mother for letting my son out of my sight like that." She could feel his gaze on her and the heat from his body. He was sitting close. He'd been doing that a lot during the afternoon and evening, standing close, touching her at every opportunity. She'd needed the comfort of his touch when J.T. had been missing. Now, comfort was the furthest thing from her mind. The casual brush of his fingertips sent sparks of longing right to her midsection, urges she had no way of controlling.

"I'm not real up on the behavior of kids, but having been one myself once, I know you can't keep an eye on them every second. I'd think that's especially true for little boys."

"That scares me," Josie said. "I read in the papers all the time about kids drowning in swimming pools or being hit by cars, or wandering off and being picked up by strangers." She closed her eyes for a second. "When I think about something like that happening to J.T., I can hardly stand it. He means the world to me."

"Sounds like you're trying to convince me, sugar. There's no need, you know."

His low, raspy voice sent chills up her spine. But were they chills of passion or unease? She wasn't sure.

"Did it cross your mind, though? That I should have been watching him closer?" What if he saw this afternoon's incident as a point in his favor should he decide to pursue his parental rights? She didn't want to give him any extra ammunition.

"I'm flattered that you care about what I think. But if we're going to lay blame, I might as well take some of it. I was there, too."

"Yes, but J.T.'s my responsibility."

"He could be mine, too," he said quietly.

That's what Josie was afraid of. But allowing Chase to accept responsibility would change everything. And she just couldn't let that happen.

"Lightning bugs," J.T. whispered, saving her from having to comment, or argue.

Josie shifted J.T. on her lap, then tightened her arms around him and kissed the top of his sweaty head. "Lots of them, huh?" Fireflies swarmed the yard, sending flashes of yellow glow all around them. She glanced down and noticed that her son's eyelids were starting to get heavy. He'd had an adventurous day. One she'd just as soon not repeat.

"Ever catch 'em and pinch the tails off when they light up?" Chase asked.

Josie smiled in the darkness as old, fond memories slid into place like classic records dropping onto a turntable. She was grateful that Chase didn't press her on the joint responsibility thing.

"Yes. I'd stick them all over myself like necklaces or bracelet's. Bobby and I used to pretend they were special, magical diamonds that glowed only in the dark."

Chase caught one of the insects in his hand, pinched off the tail just as it lit up, then stuck the lighted goo on J.T.'s pudgy arm. Josie noticed how his fingers seemed to linger on the baby's skin. She knew it was fanciful to think so, but his silence seemed to carry an air of sadness.

"Tell me about Bobby."

So she hadn't imagined it. There was sadness there. "What do you want to know?"

Chase shrugged. "Anything. Everything. He was my brother, but I never knew him. You did. You can make him real for me." He paused. "Unless..."

"No, it isn't painful for me to talk about Bobby," she said, reading his mind. "We grew up together."

"And slaughtered tons of lightning bugs together?"

She smiled. "Yes. Mama did sewing for Miz Alexander, and I tagged along and hung out with Bobby. He didn't care that I wasn't in his class of society, so to speak."

"Ah, that good ol' code of the south."

"Something like that. Anyway, when I wasn't with Mary Alice, I was with Bobby. We smoked out behind the barn when I was thirteen and fished out on the lake in a boat we sort of "borrowed" from Mr. Potts's dock." She grinned when she heard Chase chuckle.

"My girlfriends and I'd go riding through town, looking for boys. It always seemed Bobby was there, hanging out. We'd just kind of end up together. One night we found ourselves on an old back road deep in the cotton fields."

"And the rest, as they say, is history?"

Josie shrugged. "I suppose, or at least a turning point. I asked him to my senior prom. It felt easy, right somehow. We were best friends who fell in love. We ran into a little opposition from both families—"

"Even yours?" He seemed surprised.

"Yes. Mama wasn't real sure a union like ours could actually make it. She wasn't very supportive at first." Nor was she to this day, but Josie didn't admit that.

"I see."

She wondered if he really did. But it was difficult to explain her mother to anyone. Eleanor Halliday was a martyr with a perpetually bitter slant to her mouth. She always wanted what others had, and never failed to remind Josie of her "place." Josie couldn't keep track of the number of times her mother had said, "When times get tough, Josephine Mae, you'll bail out. You've never been one to finish what you started." It seemed that Eleanor Halliday did her best to project her own inadequacies onto her daughter. Josie tried not to let the negative words take hold, but sometimes it was darn difficult. When Eleanor had hinted that Josie wasn't good enough to be an Alexander because of who her family was, Josie had set out with a fierce determination to prove her wrong.

"But Bobby didn't care about what others thought," she continued, forcefully setting aside her mother's negative predictions. "He was really self-assured in that way. He made his own decisions and never asked for or needed anyone else's approval. It was almost like he didn't notice, or that it didn't ever cross his mind that someone might object to his choices, whether it be to a wife or the life-style he led."

"And what kind of life-style was that?"

"Simple. Bobby wasn't interested in being the lord of the town. He was a farmer. He loved the land and this house, and he loved people. And everyone loved Bobby. There was just something about him . . . an easiness, I guess. Folks felt downright at home around him."

"Sounds like a tough act to follow." He didn't say it with any malice and Josie didn't take it that way. "So my brother liked to fish and farm the land. Did he do much hunting?"

Josie couldn't help the bubble of laughter that escaped. "Bobby was a terrible shot. The only time in his life that he killed a deer was when he hit one with his pickup out on 133. Killed it dead."

"That'll do it," Chase said dryly.

She could see the flash of his dimples in the shadowy light coming through the front door. She liked the idea that her stories of Bobby could make him smile. Bobby would have liked Chase Fowler. "It also killed the truck. Totaled out the whole front end. Everybody teased him about it. Said for him to use the gun next time, that it'd be a whole lot cheaper. Bobby took the teasing in stride. Like I said, he wasn't a very good shot.''

"Maybe you're not giving him enough credit. A deer's a pretty big target, sugar.''

When he called her sugar in that slow, sexy drawl of his, it made her want to forget everything that stood between them. But now wasn't the time to think about such things, not when she was trying to give him a glimpse of a man she had once loved, of the brother he'd never known.

"Didn't matter. I remember one time when a couple of skunks took up residence under the car. I about had a fit and told him to get the gun and get rid of those creatures. Bless his heart, he made an heroic effort... and shot out every blame tire on the Jeep in the process." She laughed at the memory and shook her head. "No, hunting definitely wasn't Bobby's thing. He'd just as soon celebrate nature as to use it for sport, or even for food.''

"I imagine that was a hard pill for Leroy to swallow.''

Josie frowned, at both the statement and the switch in topics. She'd almost forgotten that Leroy was Chase's father also. Then an awful thought struck her.

"Chase, are you here for revenge?" Sweet heaven, if that was his goal, he had the perfect weapon. Leroy's pride and joy.

Leroy's grandson.

She waited with a sense of dread as he seemed to mull over his answer.

Chase propped an elbow on his knee. Through the spidery Spanish moss dripping off the oak tree, he could barely see the single emergency light from his airstrip winking in the distance like a beacon.

"Revenge is something you plan, sugar. When I bought the place next door, I had no idea you were here. If you recall, I didn't even know your name." If he had, he'd have come a hell of a lot sooner.

"Yes, but you knew Leroy's, didn't you?"

"Obviously. It was on the escrow papers."

"No, I meant you knew he was your father."

"I try not to think about him in that capacity, Josie. James Fowler is my father." Her questions sparked thoughts he tried not to analyze too thoroughly. He hadn't consciously labeled his agenda as revenge, but perhaps it was. He'd chosen this town because of its suitability for his business. He intended to make the Fowler name bigger and better than any other in this town—Alexander included—but that was just a point of pride with him. The injured child in him wanted to puff out his chest and say, "See there, I'm pretty great after all."

Finding Josie here, learning he had a brother who had died and a son he might never have known about, screwed things up a little more in his mind.

Through her words, Josie had painted a picture of his brother, a guy he'd probably have liked a lot. A guy she'd loved enough to have a baby for. He tried to be charitable, to understand her motives. And deep down, he did. Still, something bugged him, nagged at him.

He glanced down at the little boy whose dark head so like his own was resting against Josie's breast, asleep. In this child's life, Chase was a stranger, an outsider looking in. A pattern that had shaped his

own early years. It hit him then, what was really
bothering him.

Once again, the Alexanders had something that
was rightfully his.

The realization jolted him like a gear-up landing.

He wanted his son to have his name, the Fowler
name, the name he associated with pride and unconditional love.

And he wanted Josie Alexander.

She didn't seem inclined to question him further
about his motives or lack thereof, which was fine
with him. He'd just as soon change the subject anyway. Talking, even thinking about Leroy set him off-
balance.

"Looks like somebody finally gave up the ghost."
Softly, he touched J.T.'s cheek, surprised to find his
hand was shaking. Odd. He was known for his
steady hands. But it gave him a punch in the stomach to think that this kid was his, a feeling very much
like stepping out of a cockpit and missing a step,
finding nothing but a thin, uncertain void beneath
him.

"Yes."

"Want me to take him in for you?"

He saw her hesitation, and the protective way her
arms closed around the boy as she stood. "I can
manage, thanks."

Chase stood and shoved his hands in his pockets.
He wasn't ready for the evening to end, but Josie's
body language told him he didn't have much choice.
Still, he gave it a shot. "I guess you're not going to
invite me in?"

"No," she said quietly.

He could tell her thoughts ran parallel to his. If she let him in, he would kiss her. And it would be damned hard to stop at just one kiss. He could almost feel the shape of her breast in his palm, the silky smoothness of her flesh. J.T. between them was like a safeguard. But once she laid the boy down...

Chase closed his eyes for a moment and drew in a deep breath. When he opened them again, he saw that both anticipation and resistance were evident in Josie's green eyes, in the slight, moist part of her lips. As if to hide herself from him, she bent her head, letting the curtain of her thick, long hair shield her expression from view.

Soon, he promised himself. "So, what'll you do with the rest of the evening?"

"Sew."

He raised his brow, inviting her to elaborate. He knew he was stalling, like a kid on a first date who suddenly found himself tongue-tied. "What are you sewing?"

"Lingerie."

"Come again?" He hadn't intended the double meaning, but his words hit him that way nonetheless. He grinned and waited to see if she'd take the bait.

She struggled with it, but she didn't bite. "You heard me."

"Nightgowns and stuff?"

"And stuff."

Chase felt his skin heat. It didn't take much to arouse erotic images around Josie Alexander. He allowed his gaze to cruise over her denim shorts and T-shirt. "And do you wear this...stuff?" He had to clear his throat.

"Every day. It wouldn't be a very good business practice if I didn't wear my own product."

Chase's mind flashed on a distant memory, of exotic peach silk and sheer lace, held in place by tiny ribbons tied in a bow. He'd taken his time with those fragile fastenings, reveling at the way her smooth, flat stomach had sucked in at the mere trace of his fingertips, how her breath had hitched and her nipples pebbled as he'd drawn that scrap of silk between her legs, tugging, arousing, then soothing.

Her undergarments alone had been enough to create a visual orgasm. The woman inside those slinky panties had been pure fantasy—a fantasy he was dying to relive.

He saw her chest rise and fall, saw her eyes skitter away for an instant before swinging back, locking on his, as though she didn't want to look at him but was helplessly drawn.

"You remember how it was, don't you, sugar?"

"Yes."

Although her answer was a reluctant whisper, he admired her honesty. "Let me come in with you."

She shook her head.

"Why not?" If he couldn't take her in his arms, he thought he might explode.

"I just...we can't." She turned and opened the screen door. "Good night, Chase."

"Josie?"

She hesitated, shifting J.T. higher on her shoulder.

"It won't go away, you know." He saw her shoulders stiffen. "There's more between us than that boy you're holding in your arms. Sooner or later, you're going to have to admit that to yourself.''

She looked back at him for a brief instant. "I might admit it to myself, Chase. I'm just not sure I can admit it to the world."

Chapter Six

Sunday mornings were social, festive... and reserved almost exclusively for the First Baptist Church. Unless a person was absolutely bedridden, attendance was a matter of protocol rather than conscious choice. It was a place to see and be seen, with a healthy dose of spiritual guidance thrown in for good measure.

Josie was running late and had entertained ideas of skipping the service, but dismissed that notion soon enough, knowing that to do so would have the whole town either stopping by or calling to check on her health.

Small towns could be a blessing or a curse.

After dropping J.T. off at the nursery, she slipped in the side door. The noise level in the small church was anything but reverent as folks visited or exchanged bits of gossip that had probably run the town circuit three times over.

The smells of aged wood, lemon oil and fragrant flowers assailed her as she stood for a moment and surveyed the crowd. The Alexanders always sat in the third pew on the right. Eleanor and Russ Halliday, Josie's parents, occupied the fourth on the left. Tradition. Or arrogance, depending on one's point of view. Josie hated having to choose which family to sit with, and berated herself for her tardiness.

In true cowardly spirit, she headed for the back of the church and slipped in next to Mary Alice and Bud Temple.

"Well, I don't believe it," Mary Alice whispered. "You into living dangerously this mornin' or what?"

"I could ask you the same," Josie countered. "Ya'll keep sitting this close to the back door, Brother Mac's liable to single you out in front of the whole congregation and make you come up front."

Mary Alice giggled. "Naw. He'll just figure Bud's on call and might have to get out in a hurry."

"Shame on you, Mary Alice. Lying in the Lord's house. Besides, who in their right mind would disturb the peace on a Sunday morning? You know good and well the whole town's in here."

"They are now." Mary Alice lifted her blond eyebrows and gave a bare nod of her head. The din in the small church suffered an instant of deafening silence, like a night creature disturbs the harmonizing chorus of insects.

Chase Fowler scooted into the space next to Josie at the end of the pew, crowding her against Mary Alice, who very politely moved over a few inches... but not nearly enough.

"Morning," he said.

"Morning," Josie mumbled. Her mind had gone blessedly blank, her hands trembled, her stomach felt as if she'd just crested the tallest hill of a roller coaster, and Mary Alice didn't help this utter confusion one whit when she discretely nudged Josie with her elbow in one of those my-oh-my type gestures. Josie made a valiant effort to ignore both her friend and the virile man who'd caused such a stir by simply entering the church and sitting down beside her.

It was a useless effort.

At least as far as ignoring Chase went.

The superb fit of his lightweight charcoal suit and the clean smell of soap mixed with a hint of woodsy cologne were devastating to her senses. Their thighs were pressed together in the crowded confines of the pew, his body heat radiating right through the fuchsia silk of her summer dress.

Why in the world had she worn such a flamboyant color? Josie wondered. She felt like the main event at a peep show, with an entire church congregation as avid spectators.

Under the guise of shifting in their seats, yawning or scratching their heads, people angled to get a better look at the new man in town—and the woman he'd chosen to sit with. Josie could feel speculation from just about every parishioner and she began to squirm.

With the armrest digging into his side, Chase tried to find a more comfortable position on the hard bench seat. He knew he'd crowded Josie by sitting here, but he had no intention of moving. The press of her body against his was a position he'd like to maneuver her into more often.

He was still simmering with anger over her admission that there was something between them but that she didn't want to make it public. That declaration had spurred him into showing up at church this morning—something he'd avoided doing in the month or so he'd been in Alexander. A small part of him wanted to push the issue.

He noted her unease in the fine trembling where their shoulders and thighs touched. It wasn't all nerves. Part of it was sexual. He was experienced enough to discern that much. The realization gave him a small sense of satisfaction.

He glanced down at the silent woman beside him. God, she was gorgeous. Though deceptively loose, her bright silk dress sculpted every curve and line of her body. Soft, rich folds of material floated over her knees and halfway down her calves. A pity, he thought. She had fabulous legs, long and slender. The type of legs best shown off in a miniskirt ... or high-cut satin panties.

Just looking at her made him hot, and he shifted in the limited space of his seat. He couldn't imagine a more inappropriate place for a man to have an arousal than church.

Especially when he'd already drawn a shameless amount of attention by simply walking in the door.

And placed that attention squarely on Josie, he realized.

In the near public setting he could almost feel the guilt radiating out of her. He imagined her wondering if the whole town knew her secret, *their* secret.

Heck of an imagination, he chided himself.

Still, it made him feel like even more of an outsider.

That shouldn't be. He had a right to be part of this town. More right than folks knew. And wouldn't that just blow the lid sky-high and create a scandal that would keep them rocking for years.

Since Josie seemed to be doing her best to ignore him, Chase's gaze roamed the crowd and landed on Leroy. The old man sat rock-stiff in his wheelchair. So, the mighty king had taken a fall, Chase thought.

He wondered just what would happen if he stood up and told this crowd that *he* was Leroy's first-born. The kid who wasn't good enough. The one set aside. Yeah, well he was here now. He'd been buying parcels of land in this town for quite a few years, anonymously. Soon enough *he* would own the town—not dear old daddy.

Next to Leroy sat the oh-so-proper Inez Alexander. A cold, haughty bitch whose face would probably crack if she ever smiled. Chase flashed on an image of his own mom, a gentle woman whose serene beauty and giving nature had touched many. A person's mind couldn't stretch far enough to compare Inez Alexander and Sara Fowler.

His gaze settled back on Leroy. *You missed out, buddy. And your loss was James Fowler's gain.*

Chase felt a gentle nudge against his arm. "You're staring," Josie whispered.

"Curious," he mouthed, just as quietly. "Can't blame me for wondering about good ol' daddy."

"Chase, you're in a church."

He tore his gaze away from the man in the wheelchair. Looking down at Josie's disapproving expression, he felt the corners of his lips pull upward. "Thanks for the news flash. For a minute there I thought we were at the picture show."

"I'm sure the Lord doesn't appreciate sarcasm in His house."

Chase wanted to laugh out loud. Her prim tone was at odds with the reluctant amusement in her green eyes. For a moment their gazes locked. Shared amusement changed to shared passion—flashes of memories of all that was behind them, the emotions between them now, and the uncertain future still to come.

Josie glanced away first. Oh, boy, Sunny's Diner would be abuzz tomorrow. She could picture it now, over Cherry Cokes and Marlboros, the talk of the town would be Josie Alexander making eyes with Chase Fowler. She wanted to find a hole and sink into it, but Brother Mac called for everyone to begin worship with a song.

Great, Josie thought. There were only two hymnals in front of them. Bud snatched up one, which he shared with Mary Alice. Josie had little choice but to share hers with Chase.

She stood, her hands clumsy as she turned to the proper page. "Relax," Chase said close to her ear. "Can't do too much harm to our reputations seeing as we're in church."

"Easy for you to say," she whispered back. "You haven't lived here all your life."

He inclined his head just so and Josie could have bitten off her tongue. Though he might have a devil-may-care attitude, she knew he had deep feelings. The signs were there in the quickly masked emotions of his blue eyes. Chase Fowler was sensitive about his parentage.

Led by the minister, the congregation began to sing. Josie wanted to belt out the words with the rest of the congregation, but restrained herself. She couldn't carry a tune in any fashion, joyous or otherwise. Her mother had been quick to point that out whenever Josie happened to forget.

Sandwiched between Mary Alice's strong soprano and Chase's rich baritone, Josie grew restless and a little intimidated. She felt the brush of Chase's coat sleeve against her bare arm.

"I see your lips moving, sugar, but I don't hear any sound," he whispered.

His warm breath stirred the hair at her temple, causing shivers to race up her spine. She almost lost her hold on the hymnal. "I don't sing."

His hand covered hers, steadying the book. A devilish twinkle shone from his eyes as he gazed down at her. "Everybody sings in church."

Josie's heart pounded against her ribs. "Not if you sound like a sick cow out in old man Tremble's pasture, you don't. Now hush up and sing."

Josie hoped to heaven the song had drowned out his chuckle. "Not until you do," he challenged.

She shook her head, unnerved by the feel of his palm covering the back of her hand against the spine of the book. She kept her eyes trained on the hymnal and continued to move her lips without sound, determined to appear as inconspicuous as possible. A difficult accomplishment with Chase Fowler standing next to her, tall and proud, a slight smile on his face . . . and absolutely silent.

At last the singing ended. In her haste to be seated, Josie plopped down and found herself halfway on Chase's lap. Without warning, a distant memory flashed in her mind—a brightly lit motel room, the feel of bare, masculine thighs under her legs, a pair of strong arms holding her in place across his lap as clever lips cruised erotically across her breasts, her shoulders. . . .

"Oh, Lord," Josie groaned, drawing both Mary Alice and Bud's attention. Only Chase's large hand at her waist kept Josie from leaping back up. With a raised brow, he eased her into a more decorous position befitting a church setting.

"You're thinking about what happened the last time I had you on my lap, aren't you?" His words were barely audible, for Josie's ears only.

She tried not to react...and failed. That she had so little control around this man—even in church—made her miserable. Guilt, embarrassment and forbidden desires nearly choked her. She had an urge to run, somewhere far away, away from her memories, away from her own wants, the wants she was sure were about to destroy her otherwise orderly life.

"Please," she whispered. "Don't do this to me."

His blue eyes turned serious and probing. A look that seemed to hold for an eternity in actuality only lasted a second. Then he nodded and directed his attention forward. To an observer, he looked like a man whose sole purpose at that moment was spiritual guidance.

Josie followed his lead.

Brother Mac spoke for a while about the progress of the Forth of July celebration, praised all the ladies for their hard work and contributions toward the bake sale, and announced the various church functions scheduled for the week. Then to Josie's mortification, the pastor singled her out—having to search the crowd for her since she wasn't in her regular seat—and expressed thanks on behalf of the whole congregation for the donation of flowers adorning the altar.

Josie forced a smile and tried not to meet anyone's eye as several parishioners turned around and nodded in her direction. Acutely aware of the solid press of Chase's shoulder and thigh against her body—with absolutely no room to put space between them—she felt as if the word *sinner* were stamped across her forehead for all to see and comment upon. A big red *A* couldn't have been more apparent.

It was the most uncomfortable church service Josie had ever sat through. When at last Brother Mac called for the final prayer, she reached for her purse.

"At least let the man say 'Amen'," Chase whispered.

Josie ignored him, her heart pounding. She *had* to get out of here.

Her nerves just couldn't take any more.

And darn Chase Fowler for knowing that.

MARY ALICE CAUGHT up with Josie just outside the back door of the church. "You're in an awful hurry this morning."

Josie longed to confide in her best friend, but the time and place wasn't right. "No. I was just going to say hello to Aunt Dottie."

"Looked more to me like you were running. What was all the whispering about between you and our new, sexy-as-sin resident?"

"Whispering?" Josie nearly groaned. Sexy as sin was right.

"Come on, Josie. You're blushing, for goodness' sake. I want the whole story. And don't leave out a single detail."

"Josephine."

Josie's heart sank at the sound of her mother's voice.

"Uh-oh," Mary Alice whispered. "I know that tone. See ya." She turned. "Mornin' Miz Halliday. I'm off to rescue the Sunday School teacher from my boys. Ya'll have a good day, hear?"

"Traitor," Josie mumbled, then plastered a pleasant smile on her face and turned around. "Hello, Mother."

"I have to tell you, Josephine, it was a little disconcerting to have Brother Mac disrupt the whole service this morning in order to find you."

"I'm sorry, Mother. I was running late so I just grabbed the closest seat."

"And made a spectacle of yourself with that friend of yours and that *man.*"

Anyone listening would have thought Josie was eight instead of twenty-eight. Where her mother was concerned, Josie was adept at changing the subject. "How's daddy?"

"He's right over there if you care to find out."

Josie forced a smile. "Yes, of course." She scanned the crowd for her father and her heart leapt into her throat. He was standing with several of the deacons.

And so was Chase.

She forced her eyes away and tried to concentrate on her mother, but her gaze kept straying back to Chase. He had his hands in the pockets of his suit pants. The front panels of his coat were pushed back in a way that emphasized the breadth of his chest in a snow-white dress shirt. Despite herself, Josie found herself reacting to his virility.

As if he could feel the force of her gaze—and her thoughts—he looked up... and winked. She nearly choked when she tried to swallow.

"Josephine, are you listening to me?"

"Sorry, Mother."

"I asked you what you're making for the social. Since I'm sure most of your recipes are the same as mine, it wouldn't do for us to duplicate one another."

"I thought I'd make a cauliflower salad. And probably a cherry pie, too."

Eleanor sniffed as if she'd smelled something particularly foul and tugged at the wrists of her cotton gloves. "You might want to rethink the salad, dear. Isn't that the one Miz Inez's maid taught you to make?"

"Yes." Josie knew her tone was defensive, but more times than not her mother brought out the worst in her. "Mattie gave me the recipe."

"As I recall, it has onions in it. Not everyone cares for onions, you know."

"I like that salad, Mother."

"Yes, but it wouldn't be one of your better efforts."

Josie opened her mouth, but no words came forth. Which was just as well. She'd caused enough of a stir by whispering back and forth with Chase during the service. To engage in a public argument with her mother would definitely cause people to talk.

"I'm not saying this to hurt your feelings," Eleanor continued. "But you just don't think sometimes, Josephine. You know how people are and I'm sure once you've thought it through you'll see I'm right. There's nothing more embarrassing than having to take home a full dish that no one has touched.''

Josie fumed. Eleanor might as well come out and say what was really on her mind—that any bad reflection on Josie was a bad reflection on Eleanor herself. This obsession with appearances, of living up to the upper-crust Alexander name was wearing thin with Josie.

By darn, she intended to take that salad, even if she was the only one in the whole town who ate it. ''I'll think about it, Mother. But I've got to run now. J.T. will be getting restless.''

As if pulled by an unseen string, she looked up, her gaze slamming straight into Chase's probing blue eyes. The jolt of awareness that sizzled between them caught her off guard.

''Bring him out to the house sometime soon.''

''Who?'' She couldn't mean . . .

''My grandson. Josephine, what—''

''Yes. Of course.'' Good, Lord. She couldn't believe she'd almost given herself away like that. The man had her so flustered she couldn't even think straight.

''Mother, I've really got to run.'' Seeing Chase detach himself from the circle of men galvanized Josie into action. ''Give Daddy a kiss for me.''

IT SEEMED THE WHOLE TOWN had turned out for the Fourth of July fair and dinner barbecue. The air was redolent with the scents of home cooking and charcoal fires. Steaming ears of corn, salads of every variety and mounds of calorie-laden deserts were presented along with unlimited hamburgers and hot dogs.

The highlight of the evening was dancing, which would be followed later that night by a fireworks display. The music had already started, so Josie drifted in that direction, drawn by the familiar melodies.

The sun had long since set, creating an ambiance of twilight and romance. Gaslights cast an amber glow across the basketball courts as couples danced to a popular tune. The musicians were good, Josie thought, all of them local guys, both young and old.

Standing alone, Josie looked up through the couples dancing. Chase was there. On the opposite side of the basketball court. Her heart lurched and a rush of pure adrenaline blasted her system, making her light-headed. She quickly looked away. It seemed he was always there, either in her mind or in the flesh. His presence was like a magnet, drawing her inexorably to him when she knew it was as dangerous as playing with fire to do so.

Although everything within her screamed for her to take those few crucial steps to his side, she didn't dare approach him. Being close to him would be tantamount to announcing to the whole town that there was something between them.

She'd been avoiding him for most of the day, and it seemed, for reasons of his own, he'd been letting her get away with it.

It reminded her of a fifties courting game. Each kept their distance, acting as if they'd never met. Then, as if by telepathy, one or the other would look up. Even the tiniest break in the crowd would draw their gazes.

Trying to steer her mind in another direction, Josie scanned the crowd for Mary Alice and Bud. Her friends had taken J.T. off with them. J.T. loved spending time with Cory and Shane—Mary Alice's boys—and after much arguing, Josie had agreed to let the Temples entertain J.T. and take him home for a sleep over. She caught sight of them once and smiled when she noticed that J.T. was practically asleep against Bud's shoulder.

The music changed in tempo, a country-and-western line dance that drew her attention. The scene that followed reminded her somewhat of a cattle drive. Folks nearly stampeded to get a position on the concrete square.

"I thought Baptists didn't dance," came a deep voice from behind her.

Josie felt her heart lurch as Chase stepped out of the shadows. She kept her eyes straight ahead lest she betray the yearning she was sure would be evident. After an entire day of tantalizing glimpses and wild fantasies she couldn't allow to come to fruition, she needed a moment to get a grip.

"Brother Mac comes from a more enlightened generation," she said, pleased that her voice came out strong and clear. "He even has the boys sneak in a few jazzed-up hymns every once in a while."

"'Amazing Grace,' huh?"

"Hey, don't knock it. Jimmy Lee does a great Elvis impression."

Chase laughed. "So how come Alexander's leading lady isn't out there dancing?"

His tone didn't offer offense, so Josie took none. "I'm hardly Alexander's leading lady. And I've never been much good at that sort of dancing. Any dancing, for that matter."

"You're kidding."

Josie laughed. "No. It's kind of like me and aerobics. I can do the footwork most of the time, or the arms, but I can't seem to do both together."

His chuckle set off a host of butterflies in her stomach. "Line dancing's mostly countin' steps, sugar. Only takes the lower part of the body."

The image his words created nearly derailed her thoughts. His slight grin told her he knew it. "Wrong," she said. "It takes your head to count. In my book that's both halves of the body, which counts me out."

"Hmm."

She wondered just what that "hmm" meant, but didn't dare ask. Lord, he looked good in his cowboy boots, worn-out jeans and white cotton shirt buttoned only halfway. Her gaze riveted on those open buttons and the shadow of hair exposed. Oh, God, she remembered touching that chest—and hated herself for having such vivid recall.

"Do you do this?" She gestured toward the dance floor where the dancers were stomping and clapping with a great deal of enthusiasm.

"Some."

The music changed to a polka. Couples paired off and began a fast two-step, all moving in the same line of dance direction. Josie and Chase watched in silence for a few minutes. Gracie Jones, Alexander's star reporter, stood on the outskirts of the dance area opposite them. Josie wondered if Gracie was here to record the event for the newspaper, or for purely social reasons. As far as she knew, Gracie hadn't dated since her husband's scandalous death five years ago.

"Isn't that your friend Bubba out there?" Josie asked.

"Yeah. Seems he's been keepin' company with Lindsey Wakefield lately."

"Lindsey's a nice girl." She hadn't meant it to be, but her tone was almost defensive.

Chase looked down at her, a slight frown marring his brow. "And Bubba's a gentleman right down to his toes."

"I'm sorry. I didn't mean that the way it sounded." She always felt the need to champion the underdog since she sometimes viewed herself as one of them. Desperate to change the subject she asked, "So, how come you're not out there dancing?"

"Don't have a partner."

Her heartbeat thudded again, sending another surge of adrenaline through her body. "There're plenty of single women who'd love to dance with you." Including me.

"How 'bout you?"

"No. I told you, I'm not very good at it." She gave a nervous laugh. "I'd probably step on your toes or make a fool out of both of us." She'd love to see him dance though. Simply watching this man walk was a pleasure.

The lively polka gave way to a slower number as the soft, sensual strains of "Lady in Red" poured out of Jim Stratford's harmonica. Before she realized his intent, Chase had her by the hand and was pulling her toward the outskirts of the dance floor. "You've just never danced with the right man."

"Chase, no," she said in an alarmed whisper.

"Josie, yes," he mocked.

Short of making a scene, Josie had little hope of stopping him. With as much grace as possible, given that she was genuinely embarrassed, she stepped into his arms and dropped her forehead onto his shoulder. "Now you've done it."

"What's that?" The heat from his large palm seared the small of her back.

Josie gave a muffled laugh against the front of his shirt. "Folks'll talk, you know. Especially when I knock us both to the ground with my two left feet."

"You want to be on top or bottom?"

His grin pulled at her like a riptide in stormy seas. Her cheeks were on fire and the heat was spreading. "Hush up and behave," she hissed, trying to control a bubble of nervous laughter. She really *wasn't* comfortable with dancing.

"Sugar, when I have you in my arms like this, behaving is the last thing on my mind."

Josie groaned and missed a step, nearly tripping over his feet. If it hadn't been for his firm hold they might have both ended up on the ground after all.

"Chase, I told you I'm no good at this. I can't think and talk at the same time."

"Well, now, there's your problem, sugar. You're trying to think this thing to death. Relax."

A difficult thing to do.

"Just ease on up against me."

Ease up against him? My God, did he know what he was asking?

"That's it." He inserted his knee between her legs and shifted her higher against his body. "Feel my rhythm. Move with me."

Oh, God, her heart was pounding loud enough to wake the dead at Emmit's Mortuary. Proving it had a mind of its own, her body gravitated toward his, melting into him like liquid desire. Time seemed to stand still; the crowd seemed to have vanished. Josie's whole being focused on each sensuous sway and dip as Chase expertly led her through the dance.

His touch felt so good...too good. Each time he stepped forward, his thigh pressed between her legs, causing her to ache with longing in that tender, vibrant part of her body. Her breasts felt heavy, swollen where they crushed softly against his chest.

It was only a dance, but the sensations were almost more than she could handle. In some distant part of her mind, she became aware of the song winding down to a slow, sensual end.

She lifted her head from his shoulder and their gazes locked. In the play of shadows and light, his features were hard-edged, yet handsome. He exuded a brand of sexual magnetism that was almost feral in its ability to draw her in.

A heart-stopping kaleidoscope of images played through her mind...a mysterious stranger defying the force of a storm...the seductive smell of damp leather...strong, lean fingers stroking, touching.... *It's your call, sugar. Tell me what you want. Tell me what you want.*

God help her, she *had* wanted his hands on her body—all over her body. And she wanted that now. Right here, with this man. Only this man. She longed to feel the crush of his lips, the warm, liquid silk of his tongue, pressed against her, around her, in her.

A shudder moved through her limbs, startling her with its force. She wanted to cry. She knew she had to get away from him before she gave in to that darker side of herself she'd hoped would stay buried.

She would never be able to fight her emotions if she stayed within the circle of his arms. She could feel his heat, his strength, his arousal…and her own. She pulled away.

"Don't go," he said quietly. "Dance with me again. All night. Like before."

Josie shook her head. "I can't," she whispered and ran off into the dark.

Chapter Seven

Josie drove home feeling a little lost without J.T. beside her. Restless, not knowing quite what to do with herself, she headed for the shower, letting the cool water sluice over her hot body. When she'd toweled off, she wrapped herself in a thigh length silk kimono and matching high-cut bikinis. The slinky material felt decadent against her skin; made her feel womanly, desirable . . . and lonely.

Chase's image kept flashing in her mind. A dangerous yearning pulsed through her veins. She glanced up into the beveled mirror above her dresser, snared by the reflection staring back at her.

The reflection of an aroused woman whose desperation might drive her to the point of madness.

She let out a weary sigh and turned from the mirror. She didn't envision sleep coming anytime soon, so she wandered into the living room in search of a book.

Even after her cool shower, Josie felt hot and restless and achy, but she couldn't bring herself to open the door for fresh air. No. She needed to lock herself in. She was afraid if she opened the door, all the emotions she was trying desperately to subdue would come pouring out, released in a way that she'd never again be able to call back.

She'd run tonight, from both Chase and herself, torn between her very real attraction for him and her guilt over betraying Bobby's memory. She knew the exact moment her emotions had become such a jumble. It was when he'd smiled, holding her close in the dance. So reminiscent of the gentle, understanding smile he'd given her that night four years ago when she'd asked him to make love to her.

She'd made a discovery tonight, right in the middle of the church basketball court, with the entire town looking on in speculation. In Chase, she'd seen the best of all that had drawn her to Bobby, but with the addition of incredible passion. A lightning swift chemistry.

At some subconscious level, she'd fallen in love with Chase Fowler. He'd been a stranger then. Safe. A fantasy she could take out and indulge in that no one would ever know about.

But he was no longer an intangible stranger. And she could no longer deny—or hide—from her feelings.

She drew in a shaky breath and was just letting it out when a knock came at the door. Josie froze. She didn't need to ask to know who was standing on her porch.

The knock came again.

Slowly, as if in a trance, she moved to the door. She placed her palm flat against the pine frame.

"Josie?"

She'd have known his voice anywhere. Sighing, she dropped her forehead against the door. "Yes?" she whispered, her heart beating so hard she wondered if he could hear it through the wood.

"Open up."

His voice was sandpaper rough, commanding, yet gentle. Josie knew she had two choices. She could hide from this terrible longing and hope he'd go away, or she could twist the brass door knob and let him in.

He knocked again, softly, as if he knew right where she stood.

God help her, it was what she wanted. She'd fallen a little bit in love with him four years ago, and like a tiny seed that sprouts and grows with water and sunshine, so had her feelings, blooming overnight when she hadn't been looking.

With an unsteady hand, she twisted the knob.

She no longer knew what was right or wrong, but she wanted this night. Needed it.

In silence, he came through the door, then closed it with a soft click. In the light of the single lamp burning, Josie stared at him, transfixed by his shadowy features, caught in a way she knew would haunt her dreams forever.

"I tried to stay away. I couldn't do it."

"It would be best if you had," she whispered back.

Slowly, he shook his head. "There's too much between us." The warmth of his palms nearly scorched her as he touched her arms, rubbing the silky material of her robe against her overheated skin.

Her heart quickened as he took a step closer. His hands cupped her face now, tilting it upward, his vivid blue eyes holding her in place. As his hands followed the contours of her face, his warm, sweet breath brushed her lips, causing her imagination to go wild.

"You feel it too, don't you?" he insisted, his eyes never leaving her face.

The featherlight touch of his fingertips made her feel as if she were the most delicate of treasures. She knew this man's touch. He was a man who savored lovemaking. Slow walking, slow talking, with a slow, erotically confident hand. Yes, she felt the anticipation in the sultry air like the hair-raising static of a stray bolt of lightning that struck a little too close. "Yes," she whispered. "I feel it."

His fingers speared through her hair, scattering the pins that held it up off her neck. "If I kiss you now, I won't stop." His voice, low and rough, strained for control. Like before, he was giving her a chance to change her mind, letting her know he would respect the limits she set.

But Josie didn't want limits. She wanted another night of passion with this man, another memory to add to her small treasure cache, even though she couldn't allow herself to hope for a future between them. Perhaps granting herself this moment was selfish, even a little unfair to both of them, but life itself could be cruel.

He was staring into her eyes. Waiting. His thumb made a sweeping pass across her bottom lip, stroking, soothing, arousing.

"Yes," she whispered. "Kiss me, Chase."

"And the rest?"

"Don't stop."

With a groan of satisfaction and need that matched her own, his head descended. All her fantasies combined couldn't compete with the actuality of his lips taking command of hers. As if a powerful drug had been released into her system, she found herself awash in sensations she was helpless to stop.

With sure hands he angled her head to deepen the kiss. Their tongues touched, circling in a time-honored ritual that made her crazy with need. She felt his hands shift to her back, rubbing, then with characteristic bluntness, he cupped her bottom, bringing her up against him.

She tore her mouth away from his, panting. His arousal pressed against her belly. Even through layers of silk and denim, she could feel every inch of him explicitly. The sensation was both frightening and thrilling.

When he stepped back, Josie moaned, bereft that the contact was broken. Something was out of control inside her. She had a burning urge to climb right up his body, wrap herself around him, press against him . . . anything to assuage this terrible longing that seemed to be sapping every ounce of strength she possessed.

Chase sensed her need. It radiated out of her like scorching sun on melting asphalt. The flush on her smooth cheeks and the heavy rise and fall of her breasts beneath the silk kimono made him want to rush. But he cautioned himself to go slow. Josie Alexander was a woman a man should savor. "Tell me what you want, sugar."

He'd said those words before. He knew she remembered. Her gaze locked onto his for a charged, frantic instant. Somehow, the whisper of sadness he saw in her eyes made her even more mesmerizing.

"Please." Her voice was barely audible. Her eyes lowered, but Chase understood. The erotic message in them had been easy to read. She was so responsive, like dry tinder waiting for a hint of spark to set it aflame. She wanted him to make her burn, make the decisions and the moves, sweep her up and take her on a journey to heaven.

A journey free of guilt.

Chase knew he could seduce her into sweet submission. But he wanted a partner on this ride, an equal participant.

"The words, Josie."

He heard her sigh of surrender, a surrender born of passion. "Touch me," she said.

"Here?" His palm grazed the crest of her breast, drawing lazing circles against the silk robe.

"Yes."

"And here?" Spreading the robe, his finger traced a path down her bare, flat stomach. He felt a warm glow of triumph when her muscles quivered at his touch. She sucked in her breath as he slowly, surely, cupped her through the silk of her panties.

"I do like your underclothes, darlin'."

"So do I. But I'd like them better on the floor."

He gave a hoarse chuckle. "A woman after my own heart." He'd been waiting for her boldness. She was with him now. One hundred percent. He swept the robe from her shoulders, letting it fall to the floor, then hooked his arm under her legs and lifted her. "We'll let the rest litter the bedroom floor."

"Hurry, Chase."

"Not this time, sugar. My mama always said if something's worth doing, it's worth doing right." Stopping just inside the bedroom doorway, he anointed her breasts with slow, openmouthed kisses, watching as her back arched and her eyes clouded over. This was how he remembered her. Hot and sweet and wild.

"Chase—"

"Southern tradition, you know."

She ran her hands over his shoulders, grazed his ears, then fisted his hair. "Two can play this game."

"That's just what I'm hopin' for, darlin'."

When he lowered her feet to the floor, sliding the length of her near-naked body against his fully clothed one, she nearly died. She reached for the snap of his jeans but he grabbed her wrists.

"Not yet."

As she stood and watched, he removed his clothes. His body was even better than she remembered, strong and lean and hard. His stance was sure, cocky even. A dark, determined lord, with a sexual confidence that alarmed even as it thrilled.

"Turn for me."

She hesitated. Couldn't he see that she was aching? The pulsing between her legs was much too close to pain. She felt dizzy with need, a need to press herself against something, anything . . . *him*. The anticipation was almost too much, sending her perilously close to the edge.

He wore a look of gentle determination. Slowly, she turned so that her back was to him. She felt his hands at her waist, then her bottom. Stroking. Worshiping.

"Scandalous," he breathed, tracing a finger along the thin scrap of material that all but disappeared between the cheeks of her buttocks. "You wear this sexy stuff all the time, or is this for my benefit?"

Josie could barely breathe, much less answer. "All the time. I make it."

"Beautiful and talented, too." He toyed with the thin strap at her waist, following its contour to the front panel of silk. "Still have the peach ones with the little ties?"

The fact that he remembered what she'd worn all those years ago eased Josie's inhibitions somehow, made her feel treasured—validated her womanhood. She sucked in her breath and nearly forgot to answer as his palm moved lower, cupping her through the silk of her panties. "Yes."

"Yes, you have them," he asked lazily, "or, yes, you like what I'm doing?" His fingers alternately pressed and stroked.

"Both...Chase, I can't—"

"Yes, you can. You see, sugar, I need—" he hooked his fingers in the elastic band and slowly lowered the scrap of silk, running erotic, teasing kisses along her bare bottom and thighs "—to make you crazy."

As he stood, his hands came around the front of her, up her legs, barely brushing the vibrant heat where she wanted him most. His fingers skimmed her belly, finally cupping the heavy ache of her breasts. His lips cruised over her shoulders and along the sensitive side of her neck, while his hands molded and massaged her breasts.

Josie pushed back against him, reveling in the naked press of their bodies. His touch was torture. Pure and simple, pleasure-filled torture. "I'm...going... crazy."

"Good." The power of her admission whipped through him, unleashing a darker side of him he'd only been dimly aware of. He whirled her around and molded their bodies together, cupping her buttocks

and jerking her up against him so that every point of
pleasure aligned in just the right spot. He saw surprise and a flicker of fear flash in her eyes. Then the
look darkened to passion as he crushed his lips with
hers.

Her fingers dug into his shoulders, then went limp
as he rocked her against him, angling the kiss deeper.
Yes, this was what he wanted. To feel her go pliant
in his arms. To hear that soft, helpless little whim-
per in the back of her throat as she gave herself up to
him. To taste the hot need on her mouth. To know
that her thoughts were consumed with only him and
no one else.

Steady, he cautioned himself. This woman, unlike
any other, could so easily shatter his control.

He lowered her onto the bed and eased her legs
apart with his knee. Josie felt a rush of hunger so
intense it nearly drove her over the edge. With lips
and hands and fingers, he explored every inch of her
body. With a firm grip, he held her in place as his
fingers tested her readiness. In and out they moved,
demanding her response, wringing every ounce of
emotion she was able to give and then some.

The sultry air felt too thick to breathe. She
writhed, restless, panting, as sensations flooded her.
Her mind balked at total submission while her body
reveled in the hot glory of being taken. Deep muscles clutched inside her and she throbbed with tension.

His chest slid sensuously across the mounds of her
breasts as he skimmed his body lower, raining hot,
wet kisses as he went. She knew his destination and
thought to stop him, but the pleasure was too intense, her trembling limbs too weak.

His tongue brushed her inner thigh, torturing, teasing, lingering a shocking breath away from the core of heat that craved him most.

Her hips arched off the bed and she was helpless to stop the tide that flooded her senses. Brilliant starbursts rocketed through her making her limp with a weightless euphoria that was beyond description. Her fingers wound themselves in his hair, tugging.

"I need to touch you."

"I'd like nothing better, sugar, but I'm about at my limit." He eased back up her body, then reached for his pants on the floor, fumbling in the pocket with unsteady hands, searching for the foil packet he'd had the forethought to bring along.

"Last time you caught me off guard and I wasn't prepared."

And the results of that error had produced a son.

The intrusion of reality nearly shot the mood, and Chase couldn't allow that. With single-minded intent, he pulled her to him, sweeping his hands down her body to the very center of her heat.

He drove her back into the storm of passion so quickly, her breath caught in her throat. He was done with teasing and gentleness. With lips and hands, and at last his body, he demanded with a ruthlessness that was both arousing and unexpected.

They writhed and thrashed against the bed, dark pleasures seeking to appease and be appeased. She'd never been so filled, so heated, so high. She thought she'd soar. She gripped him as he pumped into her, holding on to him against a world that seemed to be shattering.

"Look at me."

His words seemed to come from some far-off place. Her chest heaved, as did his.

"Josie, look at me."

Her eyelids fluttered open.

Chase gazed at her flushed face, felt the power of what they were doing, as well as the risk and uncertainty. That uncertainty drove him to push her limits...both their limits. She whimpered as he eased slowly out, then in again, grinding their bodies as close as humanly possible. The fire in her green eyes matched the raging heat in his own. He needed to put out that fire in a way that would brand her as his without question.

"You're mine," he groaned, and felt pure, raging satisfaction as he unleashed the wildness within him and plunged into her, hard and fast, taking them both over the edge of an obscure destiny.

JOSIE TRAILED IDLE fingers along Chase's sweat-slicked chest. She couldn't remember a time when she'd felt so lazy, so sated...and so full of her own power. Making love with Chase Fowler was an erotically exhausting experience, a demonstration of limits that could stretch beyond even the most wicked of imaginations.

The only dark spot to the pleasure still radiating through her body was the reverberation in her mind of Chase's possessive words. *You're mine.* She was mature enough to realize that part of her attraction for this man was physical, and honest enough to admit that deeper emotions were involved. Yet she wasn't ready for possessiveness.

She needed time to think, to put the relationship into some kind of perspective.

Then again, she could very well be getting ahead
of herself. Chase wasn't an easy man to read. His
blue eyes held secrets, masked his thoughts. She
wasn't sure what he expected of her in the long run,
and that frightened her. Especially when just the
thought of his passionate skill could wipe out her
better judgment in an instant.

To continue in this vein was a dangerous trek. Although the path promised heaven, it could very well
lead her straight to hell, sucking away the fragile
thread of her acceptance in this town like a house
built on quicksand.

She wondered if she could handle a casual affair
with a man who was so deeply, irrevocably entwined
in her life.

Sitting up, she searched for her robe, then remembered it was lying on the living room floor. She
opted instead for Chase's shirt, slipping her arms
through the oversize sleeves and doing up the buttons as she stood.

"There's a carton of butter brickle in the freezer
that's calling to me. Want some?"

Chase scooted up in the bed and cocked an eyebrow. "Worked up an appetite, huh?"

His teasing caused her skin to heat. Yes, she was
hungry, but she could also use a little distance.

"Gonna disappear on me again?"

This man could earn a living at mind reading,
though in this case he was a little off course.
Thoughts of that night four years ago swooped down
on her like a hawk. "I can't very well do that. We're
in my house."

He grinned. "In that case, I'd love some ice cream.
I'm partial to chocolate if you've got it."

She didn't want to place any significance on the fact that J.T. loved chocolate, too. Scores of people loved chocolate. Still, her thoughts were snagged.

She sat down on the edge of the bed, her hip touching his. "Chase, why did you make love to me four years ago?"

"Because you asked."

She knew there was more to it than his flippant reply suggested. She could see it in the subtle shift of his eyes, the way he wouldn't quite meet her gaze. Just as she knew that her own reasons had been far deeper. "Do you always oblige strange ladies in the middle of a raging storm?" she pressed.

Dimples appeared in his beard-stubbled cheeks. "Whenever I can. You have to admit, sugar, that was some storm . . . and not only outside."

Josie sighed and looked away. Lord, yes, she'd admit it. But not verbally. Her reaction to him all those years ago had haunted her daily.

"Hey." He reached out and gently brushed the hair back from her shoulder. "This is important to you, isn't it."

Josie shrugged. "I've never done anything so reckless in my life. I guess I need to justify it somehow."

"J.T. is your justification," he said quietly. "You explained all that over at the airport the other day. I said it then, and I'll say it now. My brother was a lucky guy." He touched her chin when she would have looked away.

"I think we were both on about the same emotional roller coaster that night. I'd just buried my mom that morning, and instead of hanging around to console my dad, I'd gone off to pick up a Cessna for a buddy of mine. The plane was a piece of dirt and I'd had to set her down in a cotton field. I wasn't thinking straight that night. I shouldn't have been flying an unfamiliar plane. I should have been home, where I belonged. But I was angry. . . and hurting.''

He paused, and Josie had the feeling he was about to say more. Then he shook his head. ''When I think back on it, it scares the devil out of me imagining what could have happened to you if that stranger on the road had been anyone but me. But you were gutsy. I admire that.''

His admiration made her feel buoyant and strong. If there was one flaw in her character that she truly couldn't stand, it was her unshakable, underlying need for acceptance. But ingrained, negative habits were difficult to overcome. She still felt one step behind, constantly on guard with a burning desire to prove that she was good enough—good enough for the town and good enough to bear the Alexander name.

And now, with Chase in her life, the tightrope of security she was walking was beginning to fray. ''Most folks wouldn't consider what I did gutsy. Or admirable.''

''I guess I don't put a great deal of store in what other folks think.'' He traced the rosebud design on her sheets.

''You should. This town is small, Chase. I'm still not sure about your reasons for settling here, but if you want to blend in with any kind of harmony, you probably ought to consider the acceptance that good behavior earns.''

''Why?'' His hip brushed against her, nearly upending her off the edge of the mattress as he scooted up in the bed. "Because good old daddy holds the key to the city?"

"Yes." She shifted to give him a little more room. "I mean, no. Leroy is—"

"My father. He's not some god, Josie, and the world's not going to come to a halt when people find out that we're an item and that J.T. is my son."

Josie sucked in her breath. "Chase." She had to fight for the right words. This is exactly what she'd been afraid would happen. "Just because we . . . I mean, I wanted this, and I'm not denying what happened here, but there are other people to consider. The risk—"

"You already took the risk, sugar." This time when he called her sugar, it didn't sound like an endearment. "The result of that risk—my *son*—gives me some say in the matter."

"Chase, you promised."

"No, I didn't." He swung his legs over the bed and reached for his jeans. "Did you think you could sleep with me and not expect me to start dreaming? About my position in your life? In J.T.'s?" He jerked his jeans over his legs. "You're so all-fired worried about that exalted Alexander name, about appearances and other people's feelings. Well, what about mine? My daddy refused to acknowledge me. I suffered plenty over that when I was a kid, but I had a damned good role model in my stepfather to get me over the rough spots, to teach me about life and what you make of it. I want the chance to pass on those teachings to my own son."

She hadn't meant to hurt him, yet his words clearly indicated that she had. But she didn't know how or where to turn for the right answers. There were no such things as crystal balls to tell the future, to show her what the best course was for her son. J.T. was her responsibility and hers alone.

His beard-stubbled jaw tightened when she remained silent. The sultry air in the room simmered with drawn out, excruciating tension as their gazes locked in unspoken battle, each unable to give what the other needed.

"You wanted to know about that night. I slept with you because you were one foxy-lookin' lady. You asked and I obliged."

Josie felt his words like a mortal blow. Tears burned the backs of her eyes, but she would not give in to the weakness.

Zipping the fly of his jeans, he stared pointedly at his shirt—which she still wore. In light of his present mood, Josie felt raw and exposed. Even after what they'd shared between the rumpled sheets of her bed, she couldn't bring herself to unbutton the shirt and expose herself to him. Nor could she give him what he wanted.

Unconditional recognition that he was J.T.'s father.

"I think I'll take a rain check on that ice cream." He reached out as if to touch her, then pulled back. "I gotta get out of here before I say something else I'm likely to regret."

The slam of the front door reverberated clear through to the bedroom. Josie dropped her head in her hands. J.T.'s well-being rested in the choices she made. He had to be her first priority. She couldn't allow herself to take something for herself if there was a remote possibility that her son would be the one to suffer the price.

IN A NARROW BUNK BED across town, J.T. snuggled
under the covers and hugged his rabbit close. On the
way home from the fair, Cory and Shane had slept,
but when J.T. heard Bud say something about
Chase, he couldn't help peeking out under his eyelashes to listen. Bud told Mary Alice that J.T. looked
a whole lot like Chase. J.T. liked that idea, but he
guessed that Mary Alice didn't cuz she'd told Bud to
hush on up. It got J.T. to thinkin', though. He knew
what it meant when Mama told him he was cute, like
when she was always combin' on his hair, then telling him to look how good she'd done it. And he liked
Chase.

He thought about that for a minute as he looked
around the unfamiliar room. The toy soldiers on the
shelf looked a little scary and he thought he might
cry—or maybe he needed to go potty. He squirmed
under the covers and pulled them higher, then decided he probably wasn't scared after all. Cory and
Shane had a daddy who was big and strong and nice.
Chase was big and strong and nice, too.

J.T. thought about that one some more. He
thought it would be neat if Chase could come and
live at his house—just in case he and Mama got
scared sometimes. Chase could bring his planes with
him, too.

The idea gave him a funny tickle in his stomach.
The more he thought about it, the more he liked it.
Maybe he'd ask Mama if it was okay. Or maybe he'd
ask God. Yes, that's what he'd do because he really,
really wanted Chase to live with him and Mama, just
like Bud lived with Cory and Shane.

Mouse, the lady who teached at Sunday School,
said if you really, really wanted something, all you

had to do was say your prayers and God might give you wishes. He'd been going to wish for a tractor like the one Shane's daddy got for him, but he didn't want to take the chance that he could only have one thing. Chase would be lots better than the little tractor that he and Cory and Shane were always fighting over.

Taking his arms out from under the covers, he folded his hands together just the way Mouse had showed him to do, then squeezed his eyes shut real tight. He had to make sure he didn't make any goofs, cuz this was real important.

Chapter Eight

Chase had lost the coin toss, which meant Bubba got to dust with the turbine today. "Lucky dog," he muttered. Not that there was anything wrong with the 301. It was a good old bug bomber. But he'd gotten spoiled by the ease of flying the turbine.

Banking right, using both hands on the stick to turn, he approached Josie's cotton field from the rear, swooping in low over the barn. Bushy cotton plants rippled past in a blur of green and brown, about five feet beneath his landing gear. He'd already flown a quarter of the row when he realized he hadn't activated the poison.

Chase swore. The steady drone of the crop duster's engine failed to muffle his thoughts. It had been two days since the Fourth of July celebration, two days of reliving the images of Josie, the erotic feel of her body, the arousing memory of the hitch in her voice as she'd called his name in the heat of passion. He'd automatically assumed certain things based on that total surrender, like the possibility of building a future with her and his son.

But she'd resisted.

He'd been madder than fire when he'd left her house. Two miles down the road, though, anger had given way to confusion, a confusion that still simmered through his veins. He didn't know how to compete with her adamant protectiveness over the good Alexander name.

A name that should have been his, but wasn't.

He glanced out the cockpit, his distracted gaze following the lines of an old wooden fence that separated Josie's garden from the cotton fields. The fence was in a sad state of disrepair, falling down in places, curving as if erected by a drunk. He'd have to see about having it replaced, he mused, though he had a pretty good idea Josie would pitch a fit about it. She had an independent streak a mile wide. For some confounded reason, she viewed any help he tried to give her as a takeover plot.

Women, he thought. They were hard ones to figure.

He was about to pull up and wing over for another pass—this time using the chemicals like he'd been paid to do—when he spotted Josie and J.T. The little boy jumped up and down, waving his chubby arms in excitement. Josie stood as still as a scarecrow in a corn crop, one hand raised to shade the sun from her eyes.

The magnetic pull between them was as strong as ever, snagging his attention and his gaze like the hypnotic sway of a cobra. Couldn't she see that there was something special between them? Somehow, he had to figure out a way to overcome her resistance.

He saw Josie's arm come down, saw her take a step as if to run to him. The urgency of that movement had his head jerking forward and his heart slamming against his ribs.

"God Almighty! Pull up, pull up!" His shouted words bounced back at him from the sweltering, Plexiglas canopy.

Straight ahead, on the other side of the asphalt road, was a dense wall of pecan trees.

Time stood still as instinct took over. He jerked hard on the stick and slammed the throttle to full power, putting the single engine plane into a steep climb. The muscles in his hands and arms strained. Sweat dripped from beneath his crash helmet, slipping down his forehead, stinging his eyes, as he willed the plane to perform.

His jaw clenched in dread. "Come on, baby. Just a few more inches." Power lines rushed up to meet him, appearing in his field of vision like steel ribbons stretched across a cloudless sky. There wasn't time for panic or thought.

He was going to hit those lines.

He felt the initial resistance as the prop cut through the wire, heard an ominous snap as the taut cable whipped around and racked against the fuselage like an exploding stick of dynamite.

Chase fought to keep the nose up as the plane slewed to the left. His airspeed dropped, a loss he could ill afford at this altitude.

Jerking back on the stick, he shoved the throttle with all his might. Just an ounce more power. That's all he needed. He felt the plane torque and automatically applied right rudder with knees that trembled like mad.

The pecan trees were almost upon him. If he didn't gain back his momentum he'd slam right into them.

The cockpit felt like a tomb, with only seconds between him and destruction. He couldn't crash this airplane in front of Josie and his son.

"Come on, sweetheart. Don't fail me now." His heart pounded so hard it hurt his chest. Seconds felt like hours. Green foliage approached at an alarming speed, taunting him with visions of hell as blue sky, just above, beckoned the slim path to heaven.

Straining, praying, cursing, Chase gripped the stick and held on. The air tractor's engine screamed under the force of such punishment, its body shuddering. At the last second, an updraft boosted him as if by unseen wings of an angel. With precious inches to spare, the abused plane barely staggered over the top of the branches.

Chase released a pent-up breath. That had been too damned close, he thought, as he regained normal airspeed and headed back to the airport. One of the main things he preached to his pilots was the importance of doing a recon before flying a field. He hadn't done that today. He'd been in a hurry and his mind was cluttered with personal thoughts. He'd shot the three cardinal rules of crop dusting all to hell. Had he been on the ball, he would have gotten his entry and exits down pat. Instead, he'd flown in a trance, his attention on Josie instead of the job at hand.

He was darned lucky it hadn't been worse, but his duster had suffered. Judging by the vibration he could feel, the propeller was nicked pretty good. The black rubber marks and deep crease he could see in his right wing were going to cost a bundle to fix. Not to mention the cost of repairing that power line and the fast talking he'd have to do with the insurance people.

One way or another, things were going to have to be settled between him and Josie. He couldn't afford this kind of turmoil. It could easily cost him his life.

STILL IN THE GRIP of terror, Josie watched the yellow crop duster circle back around and make its slow approach to the airport. It wasn't until the cupped wheels had touched the airstrip that she allowed herself to breathe freely.

J.T. squirmed in her arms. She'd snatched the little boy up and shielded his view as the horrible drama had unfolded before her. She didn't think her heart would ever be the same.

"Want down, Mama."

Josie set J.T. on the ground, then reached up and rubbed her throbbing temples.

"Chase gonna come back, Mama?" J.T. skipped over to the dilapidated fence and poked his face through the square opening.

Yes, he would be back, Josie thought. And therein lay another problem. She'd allowed her emotions to be touched by Chase. A foolish, foolish thing to do.

MORNING CAME way too soon as far as Josie was concerned. She'd been up half the night cutting out patterns and she was still behind. The sound of knuckles rapping against wood brought her out of her sewing room. "J.T., don't answer that door, honey. Let Mama get it."

He was such a friendly little boy, she was having a hard time teaching him that he just couldn't trust all strangers.

With J.T. clinging to her leg, she opened the door and found Chase on the porch, a pouch full of tools clutched in his hands.

"Hi," he said, drinking in the sight of her with his eyes, both awkward and repentant. She stared at him, remembering how he'd left in a huff after they'd made love.

"Hi," she returned, feeling just as awkward, vulnerable, embarrassed over the way her body responded to his mere presence. There were so many unspoken words between them. Words she kept locked in her throat. She remembered his brush with the power lines yesterday, remembered how she'd wanted to run to him, beg him not to take such chances with his life. To tell him that she couldn't survive losing two men in one lifetime.

But she couldn't tell him that. She didn't have the right.

"Whatja got?" J.T. asked, easing out from behind her legs to inspect the tool pouch Chase held.

Chase dragged his gaze away from Josie and dropped to a crouch in front of the little boy. "I figured on nailing up that fence out by the barn that's about to fall down."

"Can I help?" J.T. asked.

Chase looked up at Josie. He saw the immediate protest spring to her green eyes. Damn it, he'd known she was going to give him grief over this. "If it's okay with your mama, I could sure use an extra pair of hands."

"Please, Mama!" J.T. danced around, managing to end up with his toes out the front door, even though Josie still had a restraining hand on his small shoulder.

"Chase, this isn't necessary. You don't need to be fixing stuff around here. I can just as easily hire someone to come out."

"Why should you do that when I'm here?" He knew she wouldn't hire any help. Her budget wouldn't allow it. "Besides, I noticed the cows are getting through a section out back and coming into the yard."

"Yep." J.T. chimed in. "And da cows comed up and munched on Mama's flowers, and she taked a broom to da big cow and fussed and...*shoo-ed* him! Go away, cows!" J.T. hopped up and down with his excited retelling of the story.

Chase grinned at the energetic child. "Well, now, we can't have those ol' heifers eating up the pretty flowers, can we?"

"Nope." J.T. eased farther out onto the porch and plucked a hammer from Chase's tool pouch.

"Hold on there, sport. That one's a little big for you. I've got something even better in the truck. Just your size." He looked back at Josie. "What do you say, Mama?"

She shook her head. Resignation. Not refusal. He'd put her in a tight spot. It was hard for her to accept anybody's help. And it was hard for her to let go of her child, to share him.

"We had a deal, sugar," he reminded quietly. "Take me up on my offer. It'll give you some time to yourself."

"Some offer." Josie snorted. The man was like a bulldozer, taking over her life. And her son's. Both Chase and J.T. were staring up at her with equal expressions of hope in their identical blue eyes. She couldn't hold out against that pleading. "I guess it'll be okay. For a little while."

Chase grinned and hooked his arm behind J.T.'s dancing legs, lifting him as he stood.

Josie's heart nearly stopped at the sight the pair made. So alike. So special. J.T.'s little hand patted at Chase's shoulder. Josie almost changed her mind, almost snatched her son back. Up until now, that small gesture had been reserved for her. The gentle little pats were a sign of J.T.'s trust, his way of saying "I love you."

J.T. became impatient. "Let's go!"

"Okay, sport. Let's get to work."

Chase turned and started down the porch steps. Josie stretched out her hand, then closed her fingers into a fist. For God's sake, he wasn't taking J.T. away for good. They were just going out by the barn.

"Chase!" she called. "Don't let him out of your sight. And don't let him play with anything sharp. And—"

"I'll watch him, Josie." The look he bestowed on J.T. was so filled with fatherly pride and awe that Josie nearly clutched at her heart for fear that it would bound right out of her chest.

She closed her mouth and nodded, feeling bereft all of a sudden. She could hear J.T.'s excited chatter as Chase rummaged through the truck, producing miniature plastic tools and strapping a toy tool pouch around J.T.'s small waist.

He'd given this some thought, she realized. He'd held out hope. Oh, Lord, how could she continue to foster that hope? The future was so unsteady. So unpredictable.

She'd been praying for a few hours of blessed silence, of time to herself, time to catch up on her back orders. But she got precious little accomplished. Her sewing machine sat idle as she went from window to window, following Chase's progress with her eyes, watching as he nailed up the fence, cleared weeds that threatened to grow taller than the trees, and repaired the water line that fed the trough out back.

And throughout the day, she desperately fought the catch in her heart at the sight of her son eating up every second of his presence, sometimes riding on Chase's shoulders, other times slipping his small hand in Chase's larger one, simply sitting side by side, their identical dark heads bent together in silly laughter or solemn conversations.

She swallowed repeatedly on the tears that crept up on her. Was she making the right choice for her son? He needed a fatherly influence in his life. But Chase wanted more. He wanted open recognition.

She couldn't agree to that. Not now. Maybe not ever.

JOSIE CURSED under her breath when the power went off for the second time in four days.

"Mama!" J.T.'s scream pierced the air an instant after Josie's sewing machine stopped in midstitch and the house plunged into darkness.

Without thought for the delicate fabric, Josie bolted out of the chair. "Mama!" J.T. cried again.

"I'm coming, baby. Just stay where you are."
Thunder boomed, rattling the windows. Before the
panes had stopped shaking, lightning arced, illumi-
nating the frightened little boy standing in the middle of his room, clutching a floppy-eared, stuffed
rabbit.

Josie scooped him up. "It's okay, sweetie. It's just
a storm." She patted his back and hugged him close,
giving her eyes time to adjust to the darkness before
she tried to move. She was fairly certain the lightning had struck a transformer.

"I'm scared." J.T. buried his face in her shoulder.

"I know, honey. Mama's here," she crooned.

"I want Chase," J.T. mumbled.

Josie froze in the act of rubbing his back.
"What?"

"I want Chase."

Josie didn't quite know what to say. Her son had
always depended solely on her for comfort. Now he
was asking for someone else. She felt a pang of jeal-
ously, but deep down inside, she admitted to herself
that she wanted Chase, too. The idea of having
somebody to lean on—to turn to for strength—was
starting to look awfully appealing.

And now J.T. had verbalized what she'd tried to
deny would happen. He'd grown attached to Chase.
They both had.

As her eyes adjusted to the dark, Josie made her
way toward the living room, careful to keep a certain amount of distance from the windows.

The intensity of the lightning grew bolder, strik-
ing, booming, cracking, sounding more like a war
zone than a storm. Each reverberation caused her to

flinch. Josie could feel the beat of J.T.'s heart pounding against her own. She hugged him closer, soothing him, refusing to give in to panic.

She wasn't sure if it was her imagination, but the air suddenly seemed filled with static. It felt as if the hairs on her arms were standing on end. More frightened than she could remember being, Josie backed farther away from the front window. Lord, it was close. Blue-white flashes arced one right after the other, lighting the yard, making it appear like daylight outside. She counted the seconds to mark the distance of danger, but her mind had hardly gotten past one thousand and one before another flash streaked the windows.

With the next deafening boom, Josie saw sparks fly through the air. For an instant, she felt paralyzed, trapped in indecision and fear. One of the pecan trees in the orchard across the road had been hit. The limb split and crashed to the ground. Flames licked at the bark. Where the rain had been relatively light in comparison to the fierceness of the storm, it now picked up, beating against the house in pounding sheets.

"Don't like that," J.T. whimpered.

"I know, baby. It's almost over."

Once the rain picked up like this, the lightning posed less of a threat. It meant the storm was moving off. She watched out the window, as the sky lit up once more. One thousand and one, she counted silently, one thousand and two...

A pair of headlights flashed in the lane. Josie felt her heart give a glad leap. Chase's truck had just pulled up, his timing coinciding with the burst of thunder that split the heavens.

She hurried to the door, trying to dismiss both the relief and the happiness she felt at the sight of him. Timing his footsteps on the porch, she opened the door just as he reached it.

His cowboy hat had kept a lot of the rain off him, still he dripped puddles as he swiftly crossed the threshold and closed the door.

"Everybody okay here?" Chase asked.

Josie nodded, feeling foolish that her nerves were stretched so taut. She'd lived here all her life and had weathered many a storm.

J.T. whimpered again and twisted his body, reaching out, his fingers clutching thin air as he nearly leapt from Josie's arms.

Chase pealed off his coat and took the boy. As his son snuggled into his arms, emotions swelled in his throat. Protective instincts made him want to soothe. *It's okay, now. Daddy's here.* The words echoed so strongly in his mind, he wondered if he'd said them aloud.

"Pretty nasty out there," he said to distract himself.

"A tree's been hit over in the pecan orchard," Josie said. "Should we call someone?"

"I passed it on the way in. The rain'll take care of it."

"Good grief, Chase. *You* could have been hit by that lightning." Her voice sounded breathless. Was she reacting to the storm, he wondered, or to him? "What are you doing here, anyway?" she asked.

"Being neighborly. It's what us Southerners are good at."

Josie shook her head. She wanted to gripe at him for bulldozing his way over her life, but his crooked smile got to her. "I'm a big girl. I don't need hand holding in a storm."

"Well, I do. How about it, sugar? What to hold my hand?"

Josie laughed. She couldn't help it. Nerves? she wondered. Or just plain old attraction? "You're hopeless. I could use a cup of coffee." With a good shot of brandy. "Want some?"

"Power's out."

"A common occurrence these days," she said, deadpan.

He grinned, shifting J.T. higher on his shoulder. "Don't look at me. I swear it wasn't my fault this time."

Josie bit the inside of her cheeks to keep her smile at bay. His brush with the electrical wires wasn't a laughing matter. "The stove's gas. And I've got instant." Cautiously, she skirted the end table.

"That's what I like. A resourceful woman."

By the time Josie returned with candles and two cups of coffee, J.T. was fast asleep in Chase's arms. She paused in the doorway, her heart doing a little dance at the sight of her son curled so trustingly against his father's broad chest.

Chase looked up. "I love the way he smells."

"Baby shampoo."

"And you." His gaze locked onto hers. "Your scent's all over him," he said softly. "What's it called?"

"Escape."

"Not tonight."

"N-no," she stammered. "That's the name."

"I know." Her gaze still clung to his. Unlike her scent, he wouldn't let this woman escape his arms tonight.

Her green eyes were wide with awareness. Awareness of him. Her compact body in snug jeans and a soft pink sweater had him thinking about heat. Neither one of them was going to need that coffee to take the chill off the cool evening.

Chase stood slowly. "Give me a minute to put him down."

While he went to lay J.T. down in the bed, Josie lit the candles and arranged mugs of coffee on the living room table. Her hands trembled slightly and her body throbbed. There had been a promise in Chase's eyes. A promise she found herself anticipating more than she should.

A promise she could not give in to.

"Looks like a seduction scene in here."

Josie's heart skipped a beat. He looked rugged and sexy in his jeans and flannel shirt. Power and sexuality were as much a part of his being as each breath he took. She probably shouldn't have laced the coffee. She had a hard enough time keeping her wits when she was around this man. "If I'd planned on seduction, I'd have brought the wine."

He crossed the room, his stride slow, sure, and eased down beside her on the sofa. He took a sip from his mug, then raised a brow. "Brandy, hmm? You going to get me drunk and have your way with me, sugar?"

She smiled again, despite herself, but shook her head.

"I could change your mind."

That's exactly what she was afraid of. "J.T.'s in the house, remember?"

"Asleep," he reminded her, shifting to run his fingers through her unbound hair.

"Chase—"

"Come on, sugar. Ask me to stay the night." His finger traced a path down her cheek. Deliberately, it seemed, he took the mug from her hands and placed it on the table along side of his. "You might as well admit that you want me as bad as I want you."

Josie tried to ignore the way his fingers toyed with the hem of her sweater. She also tried to ignore his words, and how accurately they hit the target. "People are starting to talk, Chase."

"So let them."

"Your truck's been parked outside my house a lot lately. During the day's one thing. All night is pushing small-town limits."

"Dottie doesn't seem too concerned about those limits." His palm slipped under the hem of her sweater, his fingers barely teasing the soft skin of her midriff.

"What?" What did Aunt Dottie have to do with Chase staying the night? With him sitting this close, touching her, it was difficult to formulate a thought.

"I happened to spot old Mr. Potts going out to his Cadillac about five in the morning the other day."

"So."

"So, his car was parked smack in the middle of Aunt Dottie's begonia patch." His warm palm rested against her stomach, causing her to suck in her breath.

"Surely he didn't run over her flowers." She caught his wandering hand in hers, stopping him before she lost all sense of purpose.

"Seeing as they're practically covering her front porch and drive, I reckon he did." She jumped when his thumb brushed the pulse point at her wrist. There was no way she could hide its erratic beat from him.

"That was bad of you to be spying."

"I wasn't spying. I was working. Dusting starts early for me. So how about it?" he asked again. "Since the older folks don't fret about gossip, why should we?"

"I wouldn't worry if it was just me to consider. But anything I do reflects on J.T."

"Didn't your mama ever recite the saying about sticks and stones?"

She leaned slightly away from him. "Do you actually believe that?"

He shrugged. "It worked for me."

Candlelight played across his dark hair, flickering in his intense eyes, eyes that held shadows, echoes of a small child who'd been hurt, a child who'd forgiven but never forgotten. She wanted to know more about that child he'd been, wanted to know more of the man he'd become.

"I can make you forget about the storm. About the gossip."

She knew he could. Anticipation sizzled, burning her. Too much of her life was wrapped up in caution. But even desire couldn't erase the fear—the fear of taking something for herself at the expense of her son.

"What happens when you're through making me forget?" she asked, begging him to come up with an excuse, a logical, workable reason to make it all right.

"When the storm's still there and the gossip's even stronger. When reality returns? What about then, Chase? Then how will I forget?"

Chapter Nine

Chase didn't have the answers she sought, didn't know how to get around her fears. He only knew he wanted to taste her again, for just a few brief minutes, to hold her in his arms and erase the shadows in her eyes. He wanted to sweep her up and take her as high as he could, make her forget all about safety and control and the wagging tongues of society. Strike a bargain with her. A family bargain. A bargain that seemed more hopeless as time went on.

He stared at her for one long moment. Then he angled her head and fused his lips with hers.

The contact was electric, rivaling the storm that beat against the windowpanes. He remembered another night when driving rain had accompanied fierce passions.

With tongue and teeth, he explored her mouth, letting her taste what he had to offer, begging her to accept. His heart was beating like a hail storm on a tin roof.

He loved the way she kissed him back, the way her passions ran deep. She was an avid participant, bold and unafraid to take and give pleasure. Even as a stranger, that night so long ago, she'd stunned him with the force of her need, imprinting her taste and scent on him so he'd been unable to forget. She responded quicker than a flash of lightning. That he could draw such emotions from her made him feel invincible and thoroughly male.

In the corner of his mind where sanity still reigned, he felt her slight withdrawal, felt the bite of her long nails as her fingers tightened on his shoulders.

He'd known it was coming. The protest, the ever-present uncertainty. Yet he kissed her once more, a long, tender foray that promised even as it conceded.

At last he lifted his head and drank in the sight of her face. Her green eyes spoke of passion, apology and sadness, a bittersweet sadness that seemed so much a part of this woman. A sadness that he'd responded to so many years ago—that he responded to still. Dark, silky hair fell back from her temples, spilling over the cushions of the sofa.

"I won't rush you, sugar. At least not on this. But I'd still like to stay the night."

"Chase..."

"I'm not asking you to sleep with me. But I promised J.T. that I'd stay."

She sighed and sat up, running her fingers through her hair. "I wish you wouldn't make promises to him without consulting me."

"What was I supposed to say to him? Wait just a minute, son, while I go ask your mother?"

She shrugged and Chase pressed his advantage. "I suppose I could go on home and just come back early. But if he wakes up in the night and finds out I'm not here, what does that say to a little guy who puts all his hopes and trust into an adult?"

Her eyes narrowed. "You're not playing fair."

"Aw, come on." His finger stroked up and down the length of her arm, smoothing and ruffling the nape on her sweater. "You're not gonna make me go back out in that storm, are you?"

"You shouldn't have been out in it in the first place."

He could tell she was about to give in. "But aren't you glad I was?"

Josie sighed and eased back against the cushions of the couch. When he slipped his arm behind her and drew her against his side, she didn't fight him.

"It offends my sense of independence when you try to take over the way you do. I don't need rescuing—from my farm duties, or household repairs or from power outages and lightning storms."

"Ah, sugar. I don't want to take over." His lips gently caressed her temple. "Unless it's in bed. Now there, I definitely want to take over."

"Hush." His words thrilled her more than she cared to admit. She wondered if that made her weak, the fact that she reveled in his strength, was turned on by his power and decisiveness, his ability to make her body burn. She'd have to be very careful, for with just a simple look or touch, this man could make her forget all reason.

They sat in silence for a long time, listening to the fall of rain, gentle now that the storm had moved eastward.

Chase felt a contentment he hadn't experienced in years. With Josie in his arms, her breasts pressed against his side, and his son asleep just down the hall, he figured life couldn't get a whole lot better.

"Chase?"

"Hmm?"

"Earlier, you said something about sticks and stones and words not hurting you. Did you have a rough time as a kid?"

"Yeah." Thinking back on his early childhood days was a guaranteed way to shoot his contented mood. "Before James married Mom I took a lot of guff from other kids about not having a daddy. That all changed, though."

"Because of your stepfather?"

"He's not my stepfather. James Fowler adopted me."

Josie frowned. The vehemence of his statement told her without words that he'd defended that title more than once. "Did you want him to?"

"Hell, yes. He's my dad in every sense except one."

She absently patted his leg, soothing, an instinctive gesture meant to convey that she wasn't one to judge. "I guess that's sort of nice. That he chose you."

"Yeah. He could've just married Mom. But he wanted us to be a real family."

"Do you have other brothers and sisters?" Besides Bobby, she thought.

"No. Mom had a rough time having me. She never was able to get pregnant again."

"I'm sorry."

Chase shrugged. "It didn't matter to Dad. I appreciated that about him. I overhead him and Mom talking one night. She told him she wanted to give him children." Chase's arm tightened around Josie's shoulder and he felt an odd flip in his stomach, that same giddy feeling he always got when he thought back on the conversation he'd shamelessly listened to.

"Dad said he already had a child. That Mom and I were the best things that had ever happened to him. He said he was a man whose cup was full to running over."

"You're very lucky." Josie couldn't imagine either one of her parents expressing such love. "Did you know about Leroy then?"

"No. Mom wouldn't ever tell me his name. When James came into our lives, I stopped asking. He made me feel secure and safe. I never felt the need to know after that."

Josie shifted to look at him. She felt the tension in him, knew this conversation had to be costing him. "Then why did she say anything?"

"Dad thought she should. Said I had a right to know. She told me the night before she died. A few days before I met you."

"Oh." She remembered him telling her that he'd just buried his mom the day they'd first met. It seemed that both of them had been dealing with the heartache of death. In her case, it was imminent; in his it had been final. And together that night, they'd planted a seed of life. She started to share this thought with him, but he wasn't through with his story.

"At first I thought she was telling me because she thought without her around, James might not want to be part of my life anymore."

"Chase, surely—"

"I know. That was stupid, and Dad set me straight right away. He's a giant of a man, in more than just stature. He's humble and kind and soft-spoken, a simple farmer with a love for airplanes."

"He taught you to fly?"

"Yeah. And he taught me about life. He told me that whatever I decided to do with the information Mom had given me was up to me. But he doesn't believe in holding grudges. Says it takes all kinds to make up the human race, and every man ought to have forgiveness in his heart, because you never know what the circumstances are behind a person's decisions. He let me know that his love for me was unconditional, and he was proud as hell to call me son."

"How did he feel about you moving away?"

"Rayville's only up the road a piece, sugar. I'll probably see more of him now than I did when I lived in the same town."

Josie decided she'd like Chase's father. It must be nice to have such complete, nonjudgmental acceptance, especially from a parent. "So, have you forgiven Leroy?"

Chase was silent for so long, she thought he wouldn't answer. She felt the tightening of his muscles, the deep, agitated thud of his heart.

"I don't think so." He absently toyed with her hair. "Leroy had the means to make Mom's life easier, but he didn't. She didn't have money for luxuries like medical tests or specialists. If she had, she probably would have been able to give Jim that passel of kids she wanted to bear for him. A guy like my dad should have had at least a dozen."

"Then you are looking for revenge."

Chase let out a long breath and dropped his head back against the couch. "Yeah. I guess you could say that was my plan in the beginning. Now, I'm not so sure. Revenge takes a lot of time and energy. It's unproductive.

"I bought the airstrip because it was a sound financial move," he said with a touch of defensiveness. "The area and location hold a great deal of potential for growth for my dusters. If it turns out that the Fowlers end up with more clout than the Alexanders, so be it. I won't sit here and tell you that it wouldn't feel damned good to be richer and more powerful that Leroy Alexander."

Josie wondered if that was possible. Alexander had been founded back in 1887 by Bobby's great-great-grandfather. The man was also Chase's relative, Josie realized. She supposed Chase had just as much right to power as anyone else in the family.

But his legal name wasn't Alexander.

"Leroy had no idea I'd sold our land to you," Josie said. "He seemed agitated when I filled him in on the details. I think he knows about you, Chase."

"I know he does."

Josie leaned sideways, wanting to see his expression. "A lot of time has passed. Maybe he'd like to make amends."

The corner of his mouth kicked up in a sneer. "It's way too late for amends. Now it's more a case of the strong surviving."

"But he's not strong anymore."

"That's not my doing."

She detected the bitterness, though he tried to suppress it. She also saw a hint of regret in his blue eyes. Chase wasn't a callous man, even though his words might not always convey that impression.

"Did you know the Alexanders are in financial trouble?" She wasn't sure why she revealed what the family had tried to guard so closely.

"I suspected as much when the property came up for sale. Buying into this town has been next to impossible for a long time. Why did you, by the way?"

"What?"

"Sell the land."

"It was the only way I could see to pay for Bobby and Leroy's medical bills."

"Then I'm glad I could help."

"Are you?"

"For Bobby, yes." And he meant it. He wished he'd known his brother. Helping out, even after his death, made him feel closer to Bobby somehow. But Leroy was a different matter. It was sort of ironic. Leroy—a rich man who'd had the means to do so at the time—had never contributed to his or his mother's expenses. Now here Chase was, a grown man, providing the funds that no doubt paid for the specialists and the wheelchair Leroy was sentenced to live out his life in.

Rough justice, he liked to call it, because when you got right down to it, the Alexanders—specifically Leroy—were paying him to own their property. He'd given money for the sale, yet the Alexanders were giving him back that money each time they had him dust one of their many crops.

Human nature made him long to confront the man who'd fathered him, just to say: See what you missed out on? Sometimes, he felt as if it were the driving motivation behind his single-minded determination to build his business, his bank account and his life into a force to be reckoned with.

In his saner moments, he knew his drive actually came from James Fowler. The man had given him his name. Out of pride, respect and love, Chase intended to honor the Fowler name, making it a legend that would be remembered throughout time, a tribute to a man who deserved recognition. In this corner of the world, the Fowlers would be right up there next to John Deere and Eli Whitney.

THE NEXT MORNING dawned clear and bright. The gentle breeze coming through the screened kitchen doorway smelled of fresh-mown grass and hay, a scent that strangely enough reminded Josie of watermelons. The rain from the night before had cleansed the air, making the world seem brand-new.

As she flipped bacon in the skillet, she glanced at Chase, who was sitting at the table, sipping coffee and keeping a watchful, indulgent eye on a pajama-clad J.T.

"J.T., honey, please get out of Mama's cabinets," she said absently, giving the painted wood door a nudge with her leg as she dodged spitting bacon grease.

He minded her—somewhat—snatching a clear plastic container off the low shelf and racing over to Chase.

"Go fishing, Chase?" J.T. asked, hopping up and down, holding the container out like a prize.

"That's the strangest looking fishin' pole I've ever seen, sport."

J.T. giggled and climbed up on Chase's knee.

Josie placed strips of bacon on a paper towel to drain. "He likes to catch tadpoles in the ditch out front."

"Yuck," Chase said, earning another giggle from the small boy in his lap. "Tell you what. I'll help you corral some of them critters in the ditch if you'll promise to come out on the boat with me some time. We'll hunt us up a catfish or two. What do you say, buddy?"

"Can Mama come too, Daddy?"

Josie whirled around, splattering bacon grease on the linoleum floor. Stunned silence hung over the kitchen. She looked at Chase. He sat frozen in place for a moment. Then his hand came up, hesitant—trembling, she noticed—and stroked the dark hair on J.T.'s head. Emotions chased one after the other across his face and his Adam's apple bobbed. When he spoke his voice was low and rough. "Yeah, Mama can come, too."

"Oh, boy!" J.T. hopped down, snatched up the plastic container and skipped out of the kitchen.

Josie made a great show of not meeting Chase's eyes. Ripping off several paper towels, she bent to wipe the grease off the floor. "He's at that age," she mumbled. "He thinks all men are daddies."

"He's a smart kid, Josie. He was testing us for a reaction."

Josie shook her head.

She didn't hear him get up. Suddenly his boots appeared in her line of vision. He squatted down and placed a finger under her chin.

"Look here, sugar."

Her hand stilled on the soggy paper towel. Unable to put it off, she met his gaze.

"I *am* the boy's daddy. Sooner or later you're going to have to come to terms with that."

J.T. HUGGED HIS RABBIT in one hand and the plastic bucket in the other as he peeked around the corner. His stomach gave a funny tickle when he saw Chase stoop down—probably to help Mama clean up the floor. That was good of him cuz Mama worked real hard and she liked it when people helped her do stuff.

He did a little wiggly dance and almost giggled when Mr. Rabbit's ears flopped against his face. He 'membered the storm that waked him up in the night. And he 'membered Chase coming just like he'd wanted him to. Mouse was right. He'd prayed for it and Chase was here. Just like Bud was in the mornings when Shane and Cory ate breakfast.

And they were all gonna go fishin'. A mama. A daddy. And a little boy. Grinning, he raced off to his bedroom.

Chapter Ten

Josie finished clearing the breakfast dishes. The echo of J.T.'s voice calling Chase "Daddy" still reverberated in her mind. It made her both nervous and giddy. Giddy because it felt right somehow. Nervous because the whole fabric of her life could unravel if her secret was brought to light.

She had to take full responsibility for this added turmoil. After all, she'd been the one to initiate the shift in their relationship by opening it up to intimacy. Had she really thought either one of them would be satisfied with just one more night?

In ever-increasing ways, she'd seen the attachment growing between J.T. and Chase. And by his words and actions Chase had made it clear that he wanted a package deal. He wanted her in the bargain. He'd said as much after they'd made love the other night. *Did you think you could sleep with me and not expect me to start dreaming? About my position in your life? In J.T.'s?*

What if she could never commit to that bargain? What if Chase got tired of waiting around and gave up on her? Or fell in love with someone else? Where would that leave J.T.?

Josie felt that she'd been put in a terrible position. So much was riding on her secret. People wouldn't understand why she'd deliberately committed an act of adultery. The Alexander men might be able to get away with that sort of behavior, but certainly not the Alexander *women*. And for that single, impulsive, selfless sin, J.T. would suffer.

She couldn't allow that to happen. She couldn't take the chance. And if Chase couldn't live with her decision to keep her silence, what then? Would he bow out of their lives? Because of her, would he abandon J.T., much the same as Leroy had abandoned him all those years ago?

Her feelings for Chase ran so deep, that if it was just herself to consider, she would take the risk. But it wasn't just her. There was J.T.'s well-being hanging in the balance. She could never, never take a chance when it came to her son.

J.T.'s birth certificate listed Robert Troy Alexander as his father. Only she, God and Chase Fowler knew differently.

Oh, God, she didn't want to hurt Chase, but she could never let him dispute what was legally recorded in the state registry.

Lordy, all the what-ifs and uncertainty were making her a wreck. Like an alcoholic's creed, her only option was to take things one day at a time.

The sound of J.T.'s high-pitched laughter preceded the little whirlwind by an instant. Josie felt love and pride and fear as he bounded into the room, with Chase following behind.

She made the mistake of glancing at Chase. His gaze snared hers. In an instant, amusement faded from his blue eyes, replaced by a look that was far too intent, far too potent . . . so very male.

Her hands trembled and her pulse raced. A memory, dark and thrilling, engulfed her, snatching her breath. As their gazes held, she imagined him recalling that same moment, that moment when he'd plunged into her, so sure, so powerful . . . so right. *You're mine.*

Oh, how she would like to be his. But life didn't always allow you to have what you wanted. And that in itself was so very heartbreaking. To love so fiercely, so deeply, yet knowing that it could never really *be*.

Because, as a mother, her first and foremost responsibility was for the future of her son. She could never allow anyone to place an ugly label on him— because of her.

"Look, Mama! Fishies!"

The murky liquid in the plastic container sloshed and dribbled on her clean linoleum as J.T. charged across the room, holding up his prize.

Josie inhaled the stench of ditch water as she dutifully examined the tadpoles darting around in her Tupperware.

"I believe we caught them all. Every last one," Chase said, his blue eyes dancing with amusement.

"Yeah! We catched all of 'em!" J.T. parroted. "See?"

J.T.'s distraction allowed her to gain back a measure of control. She looked back at Chase, her brow raised. "That was very…uh, sporting of you." What in the world was she supposed to do with twenty squiggling tadpoles?

Chase grinned.

She reached down and ruffled J.T.'s hair. "These are very handsome fish, sweetie. And so many." Handing the container back to the little boy, Josie made an effort not to pinch her nose. The smell really was awful. "You're a fine fisherman. Why don't you take them outside now."

"But they live here, Mama." J.T.'s lip pouted.

"I know that, sweetie, but they'll be much happier outside. You wouldn't want them to be sad if they couldn't see the sunshine, would you?"

"Your mama's right, sport," Chase said, placing his hand on J.T.'s small shoulder. "Fish don't like to stay in the kitchen."

"How come?"

"Because they're scared somebody might cook them."

J.T. giggled. "Naw. Mama won't cook them."

"Better play it safe. Go on now, son. Haul that fine catch out on the porch."

Son. Josie reached for a coffee cup and nearly knocked it off the shelf.

"'Kay, Daddy."

Daddy. Her hand jerked as she lifted the glass carafe from the warmer. Carefully, she poured fresh coffee into a mug and turned around, watching as J.T. comically tiptoed out of the kitchen, trying not to upset his precious cargo.

She noticed that Chase, too, was watching him with an indulgent, proud look on his face. And why not? J.T. was special. You couldn't help but love him. But this son and daddy business was getting a little too cozy. J.T. testing them was one thing, Chase encouraging it was quite another.

"Chase..."

He dragged his gaze away from J.T.'s retreating form, his eyes sharpening at the censure he could obviously hear in her voice.

But Josie couldn't back down. This was too important. "Kids are like little parrots. He could slip up in public."

"That wouldn't be the end of the world, you know."

"Chase, you haven't lived here all you life. You don't know—" The phone rang, startling her. "Damn it!" The knots in her stomach twisted even tighter. "Don't move," she instructed. "We're not finished with this."

Josie set down her mug and snatched up the receiver. When she heard the voice on the other end of the line, she sagged against the counter. The morning was going downhill fast. "Hello, Mother."

"Josephine, you told me you were making cherry pies for the Fourth holiday, not apple. I specifically asked you, then went ahead with my own baking based on your words." There was a long-suffering sigh on the other end of the line. "Since we both brought apple pies, I'm sure you couldn't help but notice there was an overabundance of them."

And oh, how embarrassing to have to take home a full dish, Josie thought. She'd been wondering for the past week when this conversation would come up. Eleanor must be slipping or else she was really ticked. She usually called immediately when she felt there had been some inappropriate behavior that needed correcting.

"I'm sorry, Mother." Apologies were standard fare where Josie and her mother were concerned.

"I'm sure Dad enjoyed what was left. You know he loves your apple pies."

Eleanor sniffed. "Well, there was only a small bit left," she said, a note of triumph in her voice. "That Lindsey Wakefield carried home two full plates that weren't even touched. Of course everyone knows Lindsey Wakefield can't cook worth beans. What with her parading around like she does in those tight skirts and high heels."

"What do Lindsey's clothes have to do with her apple pies?" Lindsey was in her thirties, twice divorced with three kids, all of whom—according to the town biddies—had different daddies. Josie genuinely liked Lindsey and hated it when vicious gossip passed hands like butter at the supper table.

"Well, I'm not one to tell tales," Eleanor replied, causing Josie to roll her eyes, "but just take a good look at her and anyone with a set of eyes can see the kitchen's not her most productive room."

"Mother, that's not very nice."

"*I* didn't start any rumors, Josephine. Now this is just between you and me. Speaking on this subject, though, I left the church early, but word still got back to me about your behavior."

What now? Josie thought. She didn't have long to wait.

"Turning your son over to your friend and dancing with another man," she chastised. "Josephine, this is a small town. People talk."

Obviously. Josie moved aside as Chase came over to the counter and poured himself a cup of coffee. Winding the telephone cord around her finger she turned her back on him. She felt as if he could hear every word her mother was saying.

"I can tell you," Eleanor continued, oblivious to Josie's silence, "I don't appreciate hearing these things from others. Why, it's a wonder Gracie Jones didn't write it up in the town paper."

With Chase sitting at the kitchen table, unabashedly listening, Josie didn't comment on her mother's rebuke. As to being written up in the town paper, well, Josie knew better than anyone that Gracie would never do that.

"Is there something you need to talk about, Josephine?"

God, yes, she needed to talk. But not to her mother. "No, ma'am."

Eleanor paused. "Are you all right, dear?"

"Yes." Josie started to soften.

"I can understand your loneliness. But you have a reputation to uphold." The censure in Eleanor's voice had Josie's stomach twisting in knots. "The Alexanders have been good to you. If you need...that sort of thing, well, a little *discretion* would be in order."

Josie couldn't believe this of her own mother. Then again, maybe she could. "It was only a dance," she said tightly, hoping her voice wouldn't carry.

"Yes, but you must remember who you are. Of course, I'll have to defend you against the talk. God knows, you've put me in a terrible position, but I think I can correct matters easily enough."

Josie had had enough. Her throat felt tight and her emotions threatened to explode any minute now. She didn't care any more that Chase was listening. Words backed up in her mind that were long overdue to be aired.

"Mother, for once I wish you'd think about me. Just me. Not the Alexanders, and not the town, and not yourself or the horrible position you *think* I've put you in. I'm your daughter. That should count for something." Like unconditional love. The kind of love and acceptance Chase claimed he got from his adoptive father.

"There's no call to shout at me, Josephine. I'm merely saying—"

"I know what you're saying, Mother." *Be a good girl, Josie. Don't make waves, Josie. Hold your head up, Josie, so folks won't have any call to think you're not good enough.* For an insane moment, she wanted to thumb her nose at the whole stinking town and damn the consequences.

Josie sighed and rubbed her temple where a headache was threatening. "Listen, Mother, I've got to run. I'll talk to you later." Without waiting for a reply, she replaced the receiver very carefully, then dumped her cold coffee down the sink and poured a fresh cup.

Chase shifted his own coffee cup back and forth across the table, watching the rigid set of Josie's shoulders and her controlled movements.

"There ought to be a school for parents," he said quietly. "To teach them how not to make mistakes."

When she turned, her tight smile spoke of sadness and resignation. "Mama and I seem to clash sometimes."

He nodded, keeping silent, figuring she'd tell him about it in her own time. God knows they could use a diversion. They seemed to be at an impasse in their own relationship.

She sat down at the table and rubbed at her temples.

"I notice you call her mama when you talk *about* her, yet you address her more formally as Mother when you talk *to* her."

She looked up and frowned. "I didn't realize I did that. I suppose I want so badly for there to be warmth between us. In my mind, I guess I pretend it's there, but when I come face-to-face with her, the stark reality hits me and I revert to formality." She ran her fingertip around the rim of the mug. "Don't get me wrong. In her own way, she does love me."

"But she's jealous of you."

"No." Her dark lashes swept down, then rose slowly. "Yes," she admitted quietly. "Mama sometimes wants what others have."

"And what do you have that she wants?"

"Bobby's last name."

Chase felt his hair line shift in surprise. "Your mother had a thing for Bobby?"

"No. For Leroy."

Good God, did the man leave no woman untouched? "Does your daddy know about this?"

"Yes. He's the one who told me."

Chase whistled.

"When I told my folks that Bobby and I were getting married, Mother threw a hissy fit. She said there was no way things would work out because in the eyes of the Alexanders we were just white trash. Daddy works for Leroy at the factory in town and Mother sews for Miz Inez. She said Leroy wouldn't stand for his only son marrying a servant's kid and that if by some miracle the marriage did go through, that the whole town would be taking bets on how long it would last. She said I ought to know my place, and that when the town started whispering about me trying to be somebody that I'm not I'd bail out.''

''Sugar, I hate to tell you this, but I don't think I like your mother.''

He saw the weary lift of her shoulders, the spark of reluctant amusement in her eyes. ''J.T. adores her.''

''And that recommends her?''

''Certainly.''

''Okay. I'll reserve judgment.''

''She's not all bad, Chase. I figured out a long time ago that my mother has a way of projecting her own insecurities and inadequacies onto other people.''

''But you buy into it sometimes.''

''Sometimes,'' she admitted. ''She is right about certain things, though. Folks in a small town have a real long memory if you happen to step out of line and break their code of what's deemed respectable.''

Lindsey Wakefield was a prime example, Chase thought. He'd heard the gossip, yet Josie had defended the woman at the Fourth of July dance when he'd commented on Bubba's choice for a dance partner. At the time, it'd seemed she'd been double dog daring him to form any bad impressions of the other woman. Lindsey was a looker and she flaunted convention.

Chase had learned long ago to ignore the taunts of society. He suspected that Josie wasn't quite so hardened. He didn't want to be the cause of her being the subject of gossip, but what was a guy supposed to do? Josie and J.T. were his family. He'd lost her once—admittedly at a time when she hadn't been his to hold. But now things were different. If he lost her now, he had a very real feeling that his life would cease to have any purpose.

Based on this new insight into her past, Chase realized he was up against some pretty heavy odds. He now understood her determination to prove herself worthy, or good enough for the Alexander name.

But could he wait in the shadows forever? He'd spent the first seven years of his life on the outside looking in, wanting acceptance and love and a legitimate name.

That damned Alexander name, as it turned out.

He thought he'd gotten past his childhood hurts, but in a sense, history seemed destined to repeat itself. Remembering the mean taunts of children about his lack of a daddy, the ugly labels folks had pinned on his mama, made Chase's gut twist.

What was he supposed to do?

He could hear J.T. out on the porch, jabbering to his newly acquired fish. "Losing the town's respect would destroy you, wouldn't it?"

Josie shook her head. "It's not me that I worry about. It's what it would do to J.T. To *his* life."

"Do you want me to discourage him from calling me daddy?"

He'd do that for her, she realized. At the expense of his own emotions. She reached over and took his hand. Lord, she didn't want to hurt this man. But she had to do what was right. Right for her son. Oh, God, if only she could be absolutely certain just what that was.

Tears backed up in her throat, making her voice husky. "Yes."

She saw him blanch at the single, stark word, saw the muscle in his jaw work furiously, saw the pain of rejection darken his deep blue eyes. "I'm so sorry if that hurts you, but I need time to sort things out. Right now...I—I just need some time, Chase."

Chapter Eleven

Chase stood outside of Dottie's boutique, amazed at the crowd gathered inside. He'd known Josie was holding a lingerie sale. The scandalously decadent creations he'd seen her cart out of the house that morning had sent his thoughts into overdrive.

The sun beat against his back, causing his shirt to cling to his spine. He didn't intend to go in. He figured lingerie sales were for women only. Besides, she'd told him she needed time. He didn't like admitting just how much that had hurt.

Instinctively he wanted to push—push for the right to hold her at night, to be her champion when the narrow minded constraints of small-town life closed in. And for the right to tuck his son in at night, to play ball with him, pick him up from day care, carry him on his shoulders in broad daylight right down the middle of the sidewalk on Main Street. Take him for ice cream and picnics and movies. To the toy store. Hell, even to the hardware store. To pick up the slack as any father should do when the mother of their child got bogged down with deadlines and overwork, or just needed a few blessed moments of peace all to herself.

And unless they came to some sort of compromise, he might never have those rights.

Still, he was drawn to that boutique window by a power that was more than he could control. The power of imagination... and that damn red camisole with the sewn-in, push-up demibra he'd seen laid out on Josie's bed that morning. He'd like nothing better than to peel that summer white blazer off her slim shoulders, ease open the zipper of her straight skirt...

"Might as well step on in here where it's cool." Bud Temple, looking official and at ease in his short sleeve sheriff uniform, held the door open. And Chase felt like a damned Peeping Tom.

If the sun wasn't enough to make him burn, his thoughts were. Unable to resist the lure of air-conditioning—and Josie Alexander—Chase stepped inside. The place smelled of peppermints and lilacs, a combination that didn't quite fit in view of the women waving around bras and panties and silk robes. Sandalwood and musk seemed more appropriate. The entire boutique fairly throbbed with sensuality.

"You here to keep the peace?" he asked the sheriff. To his surprise, there were almost as many men in the shop as there were women.

"Naw. Josie does a good job of that all by herself. Actually, I'm here to supervise my wife. Left to her own devices, she'd spend this month's paycheck and next month's to boot."

Chase could tell that wasn't the case. If the look on Bud Temple's face was any indication, he'd buy his wife the moon if she should mention an interest. "Seems like a worthwhile investment to me," Chase said absently. The sight of Josie, looking sexy as hell in demure white and bold red, holding court to half the town was having a typical effect on his body.

"You got that right. Since Josie started makin' this frilly underwear, Louisiana farmers aren't just spending their money on hay and seed. Got a mess of babies being born to prove it."

Chase felt the corner of his mouth kick up. There were more than a few men looking out of place and hot under the collar as their wives held scanty unmentionables against the front of their bodies. Henry Potts in particular—though he was several years past the stage of procreation, Chase assumed—was blatantly undressing Miz Dottie Alexander with his eyes.

Enjoying the impromptu entertainment, Chase caught a glimpse of J.T. ducking between a row of dresses. Without breaking stride, Josie steered him in another direction while still appearing to give her audience her full attention.

An amazing woman, Chase thought. All that Southern charm and polish. Tough as nails on the outside, a marshmallow on the inside.

"If you've got a sweetheart or sister or mama with a birthday comin' up, this is the guaranteed, number one place to shop," Bud commented. True to his profession, he didn't miss the direction of Chase's gaze.

"Actually, I was just passing by and saw all the commotion."

"Lying to a peace officer is frowned on in these parts," Bud drawled.

Chase saw masculine understanding and a spark of amusement in Bud Temple's expression. He couldn't come up with an appropriate response, so he merely shrugged. He'd like to think Josie was his sweetheart, but sweethearts went in for things like courting and hand holding. Just his luck, to be irrevocably hung up on a lady and she wasn't having any of it . . . at least not in public.

God, he wanted things to be different. He watched her move, the graceful arch of her hand as she gestured to a robe, the shiny tips of her nails as she slipped spaghetti straps off a padded hanger, the glossy sheen of her full lips as she spoke to each and every person who approached her.

Seduction. Pure and simple seduction. The customers didn't stand a chance in hell of keeping a hold on their wallets.

"She's good at this."

"Lingerie?" Bud asked.

"That, too. But I meant her way with people."

"Josie's always been good with people. I don't think there's a mean bone in her body. Ask any person in this room and they'll probably have a ready list of all the unselfish, caring things Josie's done for them. And that list would be pretty long because she's grown up with most of these folks."

She'd earned that respect and admiration, Chase realized. He could see it in the easy way conversation flowed, and in the approval and good-natured teasing that went back and forth between Josie and her friends. J.T., who was gamboling underfoot like a mischievous puppy, also garnered a lion's share of attention and accolades. With each comment or compliment, Josie beamed with pride.

To lose that acceptance would devastate her.

Seeing her like this, surrounded by small-town friends and family, made Chase understand why she was so tormented over letting the truth be known. He didn't like it, but he understood it.

"So, what are you going to do about it?"

Chase's head whipped around at Bud's question. He frowned, treading carefully. "About what?"

"Man, any fool can see you're crazy about that gal."

"Are you asking my intentions?"

"By rights, that's her daddy's job . . . but I reckon I am."

Chase blew out a pent-up breath and shoved his hands in his pockets. "My intentions are honorable, but the lady's not cooperating."

Bud grinned. "You look like a persuasive enough fellow."

Chase cocked a brow and relaxed his tense shoulders. "Got any advice?"

"No, but I imagine my wife's got plenty."

Just then, a short, blond whirlwind came rushing up.

"Bud, I swear, are you hauling folks in off the streets?" Mary Alice Temple gave her husband's chest a quick pat, then slipped under his arm with a smoothness that spoke of many years together. "Hi, Chase. Nice to see you again. Are you here to buy something?"

"Well . . ." He was definitely on unsteady ground here.

"Mary Alice," Bud warned.

"Hush up, darling. I'm trying to make a sale." She patted his shirtfront again, this time in what was clearly a caress. Bud swallowed visibly and Chase nearly laughed out loud.

"Well, Chase, are you buying?" Mary Alice asked again.

"I'm not sure who I'd be buying for," Chase hedged. Until Josie gave him an all clear, he wouldn't put her in an awkward position by flaunting their relationship openly.

"For Josie, of course."

"There you go, sweetheart," Bud complained. "Butting in again."

Mary Alice ignored her husband and kept her attention fixed on Chase.

"She makes this stuff herself," Chase remarked. And God how he loved to see her in it.

"Hey, she can't keep everything she designs. She wouldn't make any money that way. And I happen to know she's partial to that emerald green nightie over there."

Chase was kind of partial to that particular garment too, but he didn't want to be the cause of speculation. Somehow, Mary Alice saw right through him to his dilemma.

"I don't know if Josie's told you much about me, but she and I go clear back to the cradle. What Bud and I know or hear, never, *ever* goes any farther."

Chase studied both Mary Alice and Bud. They were fiercely protective of Josie and utterly sincere. "How much?"

"Thirty-five bucks, but I can get you a discount since you know the designer."

"Everybody here knows the designer." Chase reached for his wallet and pulled out several bills. "Don't bother with the discount. But if you can be discreet when you wrap it up, I'd be obliged."

''No problem.'' Mary Alice plucked the money from his hand. ''Discretion is my middle name.''

Bud choked on a shout of laughter. ''Woman, I think I better get you home. You're definitely out of control.''

Mary Alice just grinned and whirled away leaving Bud to watch his wife's retreating form with a soft, indulgent look. ''God, I'm a lucky bastard,'' he murmured.

Chase felt a jolt of envy so strong it nearly buckled his knees. Would he ever have the occasion or the right to say that about himself and Josie?

As he waited for Mary Alice to slip back with his purchase, he kept his attention divided between Josie and J.T. In typical little boy fashion, J.T. was playing peekaboo with the dresses hanging on a rack. With an attention span that lasted about two seconds, J.T. suddenly changed course, miscalculated and tripped over the metal foot of the clothes rack. His head came down with a resounding crack against a square of floor tile.

Reacting instinctively, Chase was across the room and had the little boy scooped in his arms almost before the first frightened wail pierced the air.

''You're okay, sport,'' he soothed. He felt his heart racing as fast as the baby's. Being a parent was hell on the nerves, he decided. ''Got to learn to pick up your feet when you're charging headfirst like that. Suppose you broke Aunt Dottie's floor?''

At the absurd question, J.T. immediately hushed and raised his head to peer at the floor, his little mind seeming to consider the possibility. Josie had rushed to their side, as had quite a few of the customers.

When J.T. noticed the crowd, he once again buried his face in Chase's neck.

"Are you okay, baby? Let Mama see," Josie crooned, her hand getting tangled up with Chase's as they both rubbed at J.T.'s back. It was all Chase could do not to link his fingers with Josie's and pull her into the circle of his arms. The scent of her perfume teased him, making him ache to drag her out the door, away from prying eyes. He longed to mold her body to his, to watch the motherly panic vanish from her eyes as he replaced it with hot anticipation.

He knew the instant she became aware of his thoughts. Her hand stilled against his. Their gazes collided, held, then hers skittered away. But he'd seen the yearning in her eyes, the emotion. Like Bud had said just a few short minutes ago, any fool who cared to look could see that there wasn't anything remotely ordinary between them.

Satisfied that J.T. was unharmed, he passed the boy to Josie. It was a simple gesture that somehow made him feel empty. They had a son together, but that wasn't all that was between them. At least not in private. There was friendship and passion. It wasn't enough, Chase realized. He needed more—the bond, the commitment.

And he knew she just couldn't give him that.

They were still kneeling on the floor, J.T. between them. He almost reached out to touch the porcelain skin of her cheek, smooth the worry lines from her brow. Instead, he reached for his son's chin.

"Let's see that noggin, kid. You gonna live?"

J.T. nodded and Josie smoothed his hair back so they could both inspect the red mark on his small forehead.

"Mama will kiss it and make it all better." She pressed her lips to his head, her lipstick painting a visual stamp over the wound.

Chase nearly groaned. He wished she would kiss *him* and make it all better.

With the excitement over, most of the customers went back to making their selections and exclaiming over the lingerie. One woman hung back, though, studying Chase with an expression that had his senses sharpening like radar. Vira, he remembered, of Vira's Beauty Shop. And by God, she still had blue hair.

"Hold on to your hat, sugar," he whispered. "We're in for it now."

Josie saw the direction of Chase's gaze and felt her heart sink. No, she wanted to scream. Not now. Not here.

"Why, I declare," Vira drawled loud enough for every blessed soul in the shop to hear, "that child looks enough like you... Well, if a person didn't know better, they'd think you was his daddy." The downward droop of her hazel eyes held just the right amount of curious, yet innocent expectation.

Josie wrapped her arms around J.T. as if she could physically shield him from what was about to take place. She couldn't breathe, yet she knew she must. Her gaze shot to Chase.

What she saw in his eyes caused her heart to swell and nearly break. He was not going to give away her secret. *Their* secret.

But he would give away his own.

She couldn't let him do it, couldn't let him once again be the boy from the wrong side of the tracks, held up for public censure by small town bigotry.

And the main reason she couldn't let him do it was because she loved him.

Josie stood, depositing J.T. on his feet, yet keeping a protective hand at his shoulder. "Miss Vira, that's perfectly—"

"Close to the mark," Chase finished, rising to stand beside her.

"Chase, you don't have to—"

Again, he interrupted her, his lips stretching into a wide, I haven't got a thing to hide smile. "You see, Miz Alexander's husband was my half brother."

Vira gasped. As if the ears of every soul present had honed in on his words, conversation ceased. Once again, Chase was at the center of attention, an attention that held enough censure to make him sweat.

The difference was, he was no longer a child. As a successful adult, he was hardened to the judgment of others.

But Josie wasn't.

He saw her shoulders square, knew she intended to come to his defense. She would do so without thinking, he realized. As much as he'd like the whole sordid business out in the open, he couldn't let her do it.

Giving Vira a flirtatious wink, he grinned. "I'm right honored you pointed out the resemblance, Miss Vira. This here's a fine lookin' boy." He ruffled J.T.'s dark hair. "Now, if you ladies will excuse me, I've got an airplane to fly."

THE LINGERIE SALE had been a success, but Josie's nerves were shot. As she heated leftover spaghetti sauce, she fought a growing sense of desperation.

She was in love with Chase Fowler.

Not an easy love, by any means. It was a love destined for horrendous snags and tough times ahead.

Because of who she was. Bobby Alexander's widow. The mother of Bobby Alexander's son—or so everyone believed.

She felt a pang of guilt when she thought about Chase and Bobby in the same context. Her love for Bobby had been gentle, easy, acceptable, a love born out of a childhood friendship which had grown and blossomed with adulthood.

Her feelings for Chase were not nearly so peaceful. There was nothing restful about the storm of emotions he created within her: hot, immediate, demanding, an intensive pull that kept her on the edge like a heart-pounding scream boiling to a flash point, threatening to erupt at any given moment.

And so hopelessly unacceptable that she nearly gave in to that scream.

Still she sought his company, drawn to him like a moth to flame, knowing full well the fire represented danger, but unable to resist the lure.

The lure of love.

She fed J.T., all the while keeping a watchful eye on the kitchen window, expecting any minute now to see the headlights of Chase's truck turning down the lane.

Deep down, she suspected he wouldn't show up. She'd asked him for time. Hurt him. Yet he'd still stood by her, protected her from public censure, turning the spotlight on himself.

Darkness fell like a heavy blanket across the countryside. She heard the lonely whistle of the southbound train as it chugged along beyond the pecan orchard. The powerful roar of the steam engine and the clackity-clack of wheels along the track gave her a funny feeling inside, as if her life were somehow racing away, heading down an endless track in the wrong direction.

She felt restless. And lonely.

Since it didn't appear that he was going to come to her, Josie made a decision. She would go to him. It was time to stop hiding. Time to answer that fire she saw burning in his steady blue eyes.

After all, she was a widow. She had every right to date whomever she pleased. And by darn, she deserved to take this journey with Chase, to ease the ache just the sight of him created, even if she wasn't certain what the outcome of their relationship would be.

He'd sacrificed himself for her today. He'd had the perfect opportunity to force the issue of J.T.'s paternity. But for her, at the expense of his own feelings, he'd held back. Admitted to a bigoted town that he was illegitimate.

He was a man of honor. A man she could trust.

Unable to sit still a moment longer, Josie lifted J.T. from the high chair and washed his face. Her heart pounded without reason and her hands trembled. "Want to go bye-bye?"

"'Kay."

Josie smiled. "You're always ready to go, aren't you, sweetheart? I wish I had your endless energy."

"Go see airplanes, Mama?"

It seemed J.T. was just as anxious to see Chase as she was. "I don't know about the planes, sweetie. It's pretty dark out there."

"Please?"

"We'll see." Josie hesitated for just a moment, then threw a change of clothes for each of them into a carryall bag and tossed it in the back of the Bronco. Just in case.

THE AIRSTRIP WAS QUIET this time of night, the office dark. Yellow crop dusters were angled in a neat row outside the hangar, their engines silent. The smell of chemicals and motor oil hung heavy on the evening air. It was a familiar scent that Josie didn't find offensive.

An asphalt drive curved up a steep hill leading to a two story rambling farmhouse that had been quite grand in its day. The house had belonged to Grandfather Alexander. The intent had been to pass it down through the generations, but Inez hadn't deemed it fancy enough for her tastes, so the home had sat empty since the death of Leroy's father some fifteen years back.

It felt good to see lights once more burning in the windows. Josie parked around back and gently lifted J.T. from his car seat. It seemed the excitement over seeing the yellow airplanes couldn't withstand the droop of his eyelids.

Through the screen door she saw Chase sitting at a Formica table that had surely been around since the fifties. A ledger book was spread out in front of him and invoices were scattered in no particular order. Absorbed in what appeared to be haphazard financing, he hadn't noticed her arrival.

"Looks like you could use a good secretary."

His head jerked up, his eyes squinting as if he had a hard time focusing. Then that slow, sexy smile crossed his lips. "You applying for the job?"

"I can."

He rose and held open the screen door. "Sugar, some day you'll give so much of yourself away, there won't be anything left for you."

Josie shifted J.T. against her shoulder. "I like keeping busy."

"I can think of much better ways to keep you busy." He gave her a look that was so direct, so utterly personal, that she felt her palms begin to perspire.

She didn't need to comment on his proposition. His tender smile indicated that her thoughts and simmering desire were plain enough to see.

"I'm glad you came," he said softly.

Josie nodded. "It was time." Time to stop hiding. Stop worrying.

The grandfather clock ticked in the hallway, marking seconds of anticipation as they stared at each other.

"Want to lay the baby down?" His eyes were steady, deep blue and patiently waiting. The course of the evening was up to her.

"Yes."

"Will you stay?"

"I'd like that."

He touched her hair, so very gently, then lightly passed his palm over the back of J.T.'s head. "This way."

She stepped farther into the spacious old kitchen that just begged to be remodeled, and followed as he led the way through the formal dining room, parlor and up the stairs. Sparsely furnished, the house held an appeal all its own. It had lots of great oak moldings and carved wood. Most of it needed refinishing, but the potential for grandness was there. Josie would never understand how Inez could think this house wouldn't suit. Its charm and ambiance tugged at you, a place that could be formal or homey, with tons of spacious rooms that ought to be filled with toys and the happy sounds of children's laughter.

Somehow, Josie couldn't picture Inez putting up with sticky fingerprints on the walls or toy trucks scattered on the stairway, or shrieking children running about. She'd been very adamant on the subject when Bobby had been growing up, instructing the maid to keep things just so.

What a waste.

The room he took her to was freshly painted and decorated. With a toy chest in the corner and lots of shelves and storage space, there could be no doubt that it had been made over expressly for a child.

Their child.

"You did this for J.T."

"I have dreams too, Josie."

"Oh, Chase...."

He placed a finger over her lips. "Don't. Not tonight."

He was right. Soon enough, reality would intrude. Decisions would need to be made and dealt with. She nodded and settled J.T. in the wide double bed, knowing her son would sleep through the night. The glow of a night-light in the shape of an airplane gave off just enough illumination to dispel any fears the little boy might have should he happen to wake up. It was a thoughtful touch to a perfect room.

Leaving the door slightly ajar, she took Chase's outstretched hand. "I have something for you," he said.

His bedroom was charmingly antique without appearing prissy. A raised four-poster bed of dark mahogany stood in the center of the room, its image reflected from several angles by oval, beveled mirrors, both freestanding and attached to the dresser.

"This is beautiful. Did you decorate it yourself?"

"Yeah. There's some great furniture tucked away in the attic. I haven't had a chance to go through all of it yet, but this is a start."

"I wouldn't have thought—"

"That I'd go in for frills?"

The room wasn't frilly. It was seductive. Overstuffed pillows, a down comforter, an incredible one-arm lounging sofa, all done in shades of wine and deep green on a rose-hued background. Only a man comfortable and confident in his own masculinity could lay claim to a room like this.

"My mom wasn't what you would call a fancy lady, but her bedroom was something else. I used to love going in there. She said people made the mistake of downplaying the master suite. Even though it was Dad's room too, it was one hundred percent feminine. She said that way, Dad always felt like he was being invited into his own room."

"Did he? Feel that way, I mean."

"Yeah. It kept the spark in their marriage." He'd been leaning against the doorjamb, watching her. Now he straightened, his steps unhurried as he went

to the dresser and picked up a brown sack. "This is
for you."

"What is is?"

"Open it."

She reached in the sack, her fingers encountering
the smooth feel of silk. She knew without having to
look that it was the emerald green nightgown.

A smile welled within her. "So you're the one who
bought it."

"I had it on good authority that it was your favorite."

She clutched the cool material in her hands, already imagining the sensuous feel of it sliding over
her heated skin. "Yes, it is. Thank you."

"Will you put it on for me?"

Her brows drew together. "Now?"

"Yes. I want to see you in it." His voice lowered
to a whisper, roughening with a thrilling, excruciat-
ingly sensual promise. "Then I want to take you out
of it. Very slowly...very thoroughly."

Chapter Twelve

His words touched off a riot of sensations, as if each of her nerve endings was being tantalized by an exposed current.

The lights burned low, creating images of soft whispers and fervent touches. He looked sexy and dangerous leaning negligently against the wall by the dresser. A collarless, black T-shirt hugged his torso, accentuating his long, thick neck. The look in his blue eyes both challenged and invited.

Her chest rose as her breathing changed. She'd never had a man *watch* her so intently. It was almost as if he were testing her, waiting to see if she'd stick around.

She'd blown hot and cold on him so often lately, she really didn't blame him. Earlier she'd made a decision to come to him, to explore this burning desire between them, the love. It was the right decision.

This man knew her heart, her hopes...even her taste. That he'd bought the one piece of lingerie she dearly loved and hated to part with told her this. But the nightgown wasn't the only gift he'd given her today. He'd given her the gift of his trust.

She wanted to repay that trust by trusting him with her vulnerabilities, her secrets, her body.

Easing the blazer off her shoulders, she let it drop to the floor, then reached back and lowered the zipper of her skirt.

It, too, fell to the floor, leaving her standing in her bold red camisole and matching garter belt.

Chase sucked in a fierce breath. "Stop right there."

She thought her heart would pound out of her chest as she watched him cross the room, his stride measured, aggressive, his intense eyes never wavering.

"I think we'll leave the nightie for another time."

Josie reveled in the husky, unsteadiness of his voice. "You don't think I should make sure of the fit?"

"I never doubted the fit." His hands came to rest on her shoulders, his warm breath creating goose bumps on her overheated skin as he shifted her hair to the side. The look in his deep blue eyes thrilled her. His lips cruised over her neck, his tongue seeking and finding the sensitive place behind her ear. In response, as though there were an electric current between the spot he'd kissed and her breasts, her nipples pebbled.

"I've been fantasizing about these silky scraps of red since I saw them lying on your bed this morning."

He inched the hem of her camisole up, then slowly, sensually, slid it over her head. Dropping the garment on the floor, he turned her so that she faced the mirror.

"Your undies are hell on a man's blood pressure." His palms slid around to cover her satin-encased breasts. "I like this. It's sexy. Feels silky, but different."

Josie could barely breathe. "It's a new fabric. An experiment." The design was one of her newest and one of her favorites. The innovative fabric gave the garment a remarkable fit, designed to sculpt every curve with sensuality. Judging by the tightening of Chase's jaw, it lived up to the reputation she'd hoped for.

"Works for me." His lips whispered over her skin. "I'm glad you're here."

"Me, too." Her eyes met his in their reflection, then lowered to where his large palms were gently cupping her breasts.

Each breath she took caused her chest to rise, increasing the pressure of his palms. It wasn't nearly enough. With hands that trembled, she reached up and pressed against the backs of his hands.

"You want more?"

Her head fell back against his shoulder. "Yes," she whispered, surprised that her vocal cords were even capable of sound.

The warmth of his palm seared her as it slipped down, his strong fingers cupping her through the silky barrier of her panties, holding her to him in a sensual vise.

Josie's knees nearly buckled. She arched back, her breath catching in her throat, frustrated with the barrier of clothing separating the warmth of his skin from hers.

He seemed to know exactly what she needed. Unhooking her bra, he cupped her breasts as they spilled out into his palm, his thumb and forefinger rolling her distended nipples, setting her on fire. "You're so responsive."

"You're so good." Good Lord above, where had this boldness come from?

"I can be better." As he slipped her panties down her legs, his lips rained wet kisses down her spine, over the sensitive roundness of her buttocks and at the backs of her knees.

He turned her in his arms, grasped her bottom and the backs of her thighs and lifted her. She nearly climbed up his body as she sought to appease the torturous ache between her legs. If she'd been capable of a single, coherent thought, she might have wondered at the complete loss of rational dignity, but here, at this moment, all she could think about was the incredible power of her mounting desire, her incredible love for this man.

As he carried her toward the overstuffed chaise, each step he took created a delicious friction of denim against her naked flesh. Josie gripped him with her legs, pressing harder. She couldn't get close enough. She felt an edge of madness steel over her, urgency, sharp and impatient, as she rained kisses on his lips, his jaw, his neck.

"Easy, baby." He rocked her against him, hard and sweet, for the briefest of moments, then lowered her to the couch and stood back.

"Chase...?"

"Now that I've got you here...in my house, I don't want to rush." He pulled his shirt over his head and let it drop to the floor. Muscles rippled and flexed as he slowly undid the button of his jeans. Her heart pounded, pumping blood through her veins, making her throb in every secret pulse point. This waiting was pure agony. Never had she experienced this overwhelming fierceness of desire.

Nor had any man ever looked at her the way Chase did, with fierce sexual longing and absolute determination, as if she were his every heart's desire. Even in her marriage, she'd clearly been the one who did the wanting, keeping a subconsciously sensual vigil, watching for that subtle switch that would indicate her husband was in the mood.

With Chase, she didn't have to wonder. He took her over, dominated her, demanded a surrender she was more than willing to give.

It was both thrilling and liberating, renewing her faith in her womanhood.

Her anticipation grew as he lowered his zipper and shed his pants. He had the body of a god. Lean, powerful and hard. Dark hair covered his chest and surrounded his sex, making her ache to touch, to lose herself in his splendid masculinity.

He came to her then, kneeling between her thighs, running his hands and mouth over every inch of her sensitized skin, slowly, seductively. "You are so beautiful. I want to hold you like this always."

She inhaled sharply as his lips gently pressed against her stomach, then moved lower. She had a fleeting thought about the raw emotion in his voice, the reverence, the absolute sincerity, as if she were the most cherished prize a man could ever hope for. But then her mind went blank of everything except the wild explosion of heat that suddenly consumed her. He brought her so far so fast she nearly fainted. Release shuddered through her again and again, yet he gave her no respite, taking her higher and higher on a journey she begged him to never end.

As sanity flirted with the edges of her mind, she became aware of the hot, turgid length of his manhood pressed against her thigh. Her body burned and suddenly it became of utmost importance to return this incredible gift, to show him a depth of pleasure that would rock his soul as hers had been. She reached for him, wrapping her fingers around his thick masculinity.

His hips bucked and he raised to give her more freedom. "I want you."

"I know," she said, shifting, switching their positions, pressing him back against the rolled arm of the chaise. "But not yet." She held him in the palm of her hand then placed her lips at his velvet tip.

His stomach dipped and his breath hissed out. "Oh, Josie."

She pleasured him in a way she'd never pleasured a man, guided by instincts, burning passion and the gentle pressure of his hand buried in the thick strands of her hair.

She poured every bit of her love for him into her actions, her touch, her intimate kisses, telling him without words that he was her hero, telling him just what his sacrifice had meant.

Unabashedly, she tested his limits...and found them. With a swiftness that made her breath catch in her throat, he lifted her, shifting their positions so she lay flat against the couch. She saw his muscles tremble as he lowered himself over her and buried himself inside her in one determined stroke.

He filled her completely, to the end of her womb and clear through to her soul, setting off sparks of incredible sensations that burst through her in a powerful, pounding climax. Her long nails bit into his shoulders, seeking an anchor in the turbulent storm as flesh slapped against flesh, as each wave of desire peaked only to be replaced with an even stronger one, as she urged him higher, faster. She rode those waves, and when they finally crested, Josie knew she'd been given that rare, blissful glimpse of paradise.

"GOOD HEAVENS," Josie mumbled when her breath had returned. "In a minute I'm going to have the good sense to be embarrassed about this."

"Your good sense is one of the first things I noticed about you, sugar, and I'd take it as a personal insult if you got embarrassed." His arms tightened possessively around her waist as he pulled her down to lie spoon fashion against the cushions of the couch.

Josie smiled. "You call it good sense to pick up a total stranger on the highway?"

"Absolutely. Especially since that stranger was me."

She loved his confidence, his damn-the-consequences attitude. Sated, with his arms around her, she felt safe and very special, as though she could be anybody she wanted to be. He had a way of making the real world disappear, of wrapping her in a blanket of euphoria that defied any threat of uncertainty, of the need to present a good front or to worry about the opinion or judgment of others.

But they couldn't stay naked and insulated forever. The world would intrude as life marched along its course with the helpless ticking of time. Feelings would get hurt. Hearts would get broken. Duty and honor toward family would still guide the actions and decisions in the world of small-town life. For the lucky, those decisions would bring great joy. For others, a profound sadness.

"I'm sorry about today," she whispered, her grip tightening on his arm. "About Vira putting you on the spot like that."

"Why?" His open palm made lazy passes along the smooth plane of her stomach. "The family skeletons were bound to come out sooner or later."

"But not like that, Chase. I know you were uncomfortable, even hurt."

He shrugged, neither agreeing nor denying. "You can't take on all the world's problems, sugar."

But she would have taken on his, she realized. The instant of dead silence in the boutique had surrounded her as if a pack of hungry wolves had been lurking just out of sight, waiting for an opening to pounce, to shred both body and soul, rip away the fabric of peace in a way that could never be repaired.

She'd felt exposed by the threat. But not for herself. For Chase.

"Sometimes I hate small towns...everybody knowing everybody else's business. It's like living in a fishbowl." She felt his arms tighten around her in comfort, yet instead of comfort, she felt despair.

For an insane moment, Josie's mind flashed on a picture of what could be a perfect life, a perfect solution. "We could move away. Start over where nobody knows us." The minute she said the words, she regretted them.

"No. My business is here. I've dumped a lot of money into this place and I plan to build a future. And you're not a quitter, Josie. Aside from that night you left me high and dry, you're not a woman who runs at the first sign of trouble."

He was right, of course. Although she might have made concessions along the way for the sake of harmony, she'd always faced her adversaries head on. It was just that she was so damned afraid of life intruding, sucking away the bliss she felt right now. She didn't want the feeling ever to end.

She turned in Chase's arms, holding him with a desperation she refused to censor. If he noticed anything amiss, he didn't comment. Jasmine-scented breezes wafted through the open plantation shutters, whispering over her naked skin. An owl hooted in the night, followed by the desperate, lonely call of a meadowlark seeking his mate. Josie felt a strange sadness building inside her, a premonition of dark shadows lurking.

"Make love to me," she whispered. Her throat ached with undefined emotions as he returned her fierce hug.

"All night, baby," he agreed. "All night." He stood and lifted her in his arms. "But this talk about leavin' town's got me a little spooked. I think I'll hedge my bets and get you in my bed." He grinned down at her. "Under certain circumstances, a man's not above a little bondage. And I guarantee you those posts are mighty sturdy."

Although he teased her with hot words and heady promises, he laid her down against the cool sheets of his bed as if she were made of the most precious, fragile glass. His deep blue eyes held a tender, quiet sense of understanding as if he'd looked into her soul and seen every secret, every triumph and every failure.

And when at last he made love to her, there were no bonds to restrain her, no frenzied aggression to possess or hold or brand—only a poignant gentleness that nearly brought her to tears.

WHEN CHASE WOKE UP the next morning he was alone. "Not again," he groaned. "I should have gone with my instincts and tied that woman up." Muscles tensed, gut clenched, he swung his legs over the side of the bed.

That was when he heard the unmistakable sound of a child's laughter. It was like incredibly soothing music, pouring a heady sense of well-being through his charged body. He hadn't realized the thought of Josie walking out of his life would affect him so violently. Last night, with her impulsive suggestion of moving away, she'd given him hope that they might share a future. It was a tenuous hope, but he grasped it like a sky diver grips the cord of a parachute.

For too long he'd been empty and hadn't even known it. He felt as if he'd been drifting all these years, waiting for something, yet not knowing just what.

And now he'd found it. On a lonely highway, some four years back, with a woman whose passions ran deeper than the murky waters of the bayou, who wouldn't think of asking anything for herself, yet would give the world to anyone else who asked.

She had spirit and incredible courage. He knew she could take care of herself perfectly fine, yet he wanted to apply for the position, keep her by his side, fill this old Victorian house with laughter and love, do as good a job raising his son as James Fowler had done with him.

And now that she'd come to him, openly, freely, he figured he just might get his wish.

Chase was sure he had at least a hundred things to do today, but he couldn't remember a single one of them except for his need to see Josie. He felt full, bursting almost. He had a family. A son. A woman who was all his dreams wrapped up in one tidy, beautiful package.

He showered and dressed, then grabbed a mug of coffee on his way out the door. Josie was sitting on the porch steps, watching as J.T. chased a frog in the dew-drenched grass.

"Good morning." He bent down to press his lips against her glossy mouth. Her skin smelled of her signature perfume—*Escape.*

"Good morning."

"I'm going to have to buy you a new perfume," he said darkly.

Her eyes widened. "Why? You don't like it?"

"It smells great. Sexy. It's the name I object to. I don't like the idea of you escaping, sugar, which is exactly what I thought had happened when you weren't in my bed this morning."

She seemed almost embarrassed and that made Chase smile. "J.T. gets up early," she explained, looking everywhere except at him.

Her eyelashes, naturally dark, were enhanced by mascara. A subtle blending of brown shadow brought out the vivid green of her eyes. She was one sexy, well put together lady. He sat down beside her on the porch steps. "I'm glad you're still here. If you hadn't been, you can be sure I'd have tracked you down. Then I *would* have followed through on that fantasy I told you about."

"Chase! Hush!"

He laughed at her heightened color and cocked his brow. "You're thinking about the possibilities, aren't you? If pressed, I imagine I could rustle up a scarf or two."

"You are bad."

"That's not what you said last night," he whispered, unable to resist the lure of her delicate earlobe.

J.T. caught sight of them and squealed, his little legs pumping as he charged toward the porch. "Go see airplanes now? Please?"

Chase had to abandon the sensual temptation of Josie's delicate skin as J.T. hurled himself into his arms at full toddler speed. "Whoa there, sport." He shifted the child on his knee, loving the unique, little boy smell that surrounded him. "What's your hurry?"

"Mama said we haf'ta wait. Are we done waiting?"

Chase looked at Josie for clarification, but his heart nearly melted as he felt J.T.'s little palm inch up the side of his cheek, forcing his gaze back. He looked into the child's solemn blue eyes. His own eyes.

"I mind real good. And I don't touch nuffin."

Chase could tell J.T. was repeating part of a lecture Josie had obviously given him about how little boys should conduct themselves at an airport. He grinned, resisting the urge to hug the child fiercely. "So you want to go see my planes?"

"Yep." Innocent blue eyes danced with barely contained excitement. "But just for two minutes cuz Mama has ta do lots of busywork."

"Two minutes, huh?" He caught J.T.'s swinging foot before it had a chance to accidentally connect with any delicate parts, amazed at how the kidsize Reebok fit in the palm of his hand. "I don't know if that's enough time. How about if we make it four minutes and we'll talk Bubba into throwing in a carton of doughnuts in the bargain."

J.T. seemed to calculate the additional time, decided it was even better and looked at Josie hopefully. " 'Kay, Mama?"

"Are you sure you don't mind?" she asked Chase.

"Sugar, there's one trait all pilots have in common. We love to show off our airplanes."

JOSIE LEANED AGAINST the metal hangar door and watched as Chase patiently pointed out all the highlights of the brightly colored airplanes to his son.

His son.

Lord, watching them together, it was so blatantly obvious that they were related it made her ache. By now, the majority of the town would be talking about J.T.'s "uncle." Vira would see to it. How soon would it be before someone decided to probe deeper?

J.T., his small hands clasped behind his back, followed Chase's every step, trying his best to mimic the man who was fast becoming his hero.

The attachment had grown too strong to break. Someone was probably going to get hurt. And she had an idea it might not just be her son.

She tore her gaze away from Chase and J.T. as Junior Watkins strolled into the hangar. "Ya got a phone call," he said.

Chase—who'd lifted J.T. so the child could touch the propeller of the plane—turned at Junior's announcement and headed in their direction.

"Not you, boss. Phone's for Josie."

"For me?" Who in the world would track her down here? She felt a punch of guilt, like a teenager who'd been caught sneaking out the window in the middle of the night.

"Yeah. It's Mary Alice Temple. You can use the extension over there by the workbench."

Josie rushed into the cool shade of the hangar. She had to reach around dismantled engine parts to get to the phone. "Mary Alice?"

"Lord, Josie, I'm sorry to bother you," Mary Alice said.

"What's wrong?"

"Mattie called. I guess they've been looking for you all over town and Mattie figured I'd be the one to know your whereabouts."

Josie's heart and stomach changed places. "Who's been looking for me?" All over town? My Lord, she didn't even want to consider those consequences.

"Leroy. He's had another stroke—"

"But I just saw him yesterday." And he'd looked bad, she remembered.

"It happened after supper. But calm down. It was a mild one. He's asking for you, though, and Mattie seems to think it's fairly urgent."

"Okay, I'll—"

"There's one more thing I'm supposed to pass on."

"What?" Josie could hear the hesitation and curiosity in her friend's voice.

"Mattie said you're to be sure to bring Chase Fowler with you. She was adamant about that." The Alexanders' maid didn't often get adamant about anything, but when she did, it was best to heed her words.

It took a moment for Josie to find her voice. Her gaze cut to Chase. He stood a few feet away, holding J.T. in his arms, a concerned look on his face. She turned her back to him. "What's going on, Mary Alice?"

"I don't know, kiddo. I thought maybe you could tell me." When Josie didn't answer right away, Mary Alice said softly, "You know I'm here for you. Anytime."

Yes. Josie knew Mary Alice was a friend she could always count on. "We'll get together soon. I promise."

"Okay. And there's one more, really small thing."

Josie didn't like that tone. It reminded her of the time Mary Alice had talked her into going on a blind date with Bud's cousin—and neglected to tell her that Harvey Penter was three inches shorter than Josie, had gross pimples all over his face and an obnoxious penchant for trying to imitate an octopus. "How small, Mary Alice?"

"I called your mother."

"Oh, no."

"Oh, yes. And I'm so sorry. I swear to God, I prayed He'd add three inches of fat to my thighs as penance for that awful blunder."

Josie laughed despite the circumstances. "Your thighs are safe, Mary Alice. If the situation was reversed, I'd have called your mom, too."

"Bless your heart. Call me soon, hear?"

"I will."

Josie hung up the phone and turned to Chase. One of his dark brows was raised. Seeing the gesture, J.T. tried his best to imitate it.

"Your friend called to talk about her thighs?" Chase asked.

Josie shook her head. "Leroy had another stroke." She watched him carefully, noticing the barest hint of muscles tightening in the forearm that so easily held her son.

"You should go to him then."

"Yes." She smoothed her damp palm against her jeans. "But he wants to see you, too."

Carefully, with great control it seemed, Chase set J.T. on his feet. "I'm busy today."

"Chase, he's had another stroke."

"So you said." His fingers absently stroked the top of J.T.'s head, his expression closed.

"Evidently this is important. Any added stress or agitation can't be good for him."

"Still pleading good old Leroy's case, huh, sugar? You ought to know by now I don't bow to guilt."

She didn't want to coerce him by guilt. But she did want him to see the side of Leroy that she knew. The good side. When a person stared death in the face, he generally starting thinking about the people he owed amends to. She had an idea that was part of Leroy's purpose. For some reason, it seemed very important to her that Leroy and Chase make amends.

On the other hand, there would be a lot less speculation if she showed up at Leroy's bedside alone, pleading ignorance about Chase Fowler's whereabouts. To bring him with her would be tantamount to advertising their close relationship, leaving her wide-open for questions she'd just as soon not have to answer.

Since Leroy had asked for Chase, Josie felt it was her family duty to see that he showed up.

"You can't avoid him forever, you know. He's dying, Chase. You need to face him."

"Well, aren't you a fine one to preach about facing facts? Especially about fathers and their sons."

Both his tone and his words hurt, all the more so because he was right. Emotions backed up in her throat, fear, worry, desolation. She turned away, but he stopped her by placing a hand on her shoulder.

"I'm sorry."

She shook her head. "No need. You're right."

"What I am is plain old scared, and I'm taking it out on you."

She turned back to him, searching his features. "Then you'll go?"

He bent and lifted J.T. in his arms. "Yeah. I'll go."

Chapter Thirteen

Chase parked his truck behind Josie's Bronco in the circular driveway. He'd wanted the freedom of having his own vehicle there in case things didn't go well.

The sweet smell of roses from the profusion of bushes in the garden drifted on the breeze as he waited for Josie to untangle J.T. from his car seat. Now that he was here, Chase felt uneasy. He'd thought to have this meeting on his own terms, in his own time. But Leroy's health had preempted him. Typical.

All the way to the front door, Josie kept looking at him in concern, but he didn't feel like breaking his silence. Too many emotions were swimming in his head and in his gut to trust himself with civil conversation.

The massive door swung open before they'd even knocked.

"Lord have mercy, child, there's mighty big troubles in this here house." Chase stood back as the maid—Mattie, he suspected—enveloped Josie with her hefty, flour dusted arms. To his utter surprise, she treated him to the same show of affection, reaching for him before he could think to step back.

"And you'd be Mister Chase. I'd a knowed you in a minute."

"Chase, this is Mattie," Josie introduced. "She practically raised both Bobby and me."

"No need for fancy introductions." Mattie's voice fairly boomed. "Everybody knows Mattie. Come on in here. But mind now, ya'll step quietlike cause Miz Alexander, she's a hoppin' mad and don't care no hows who knows about it. Ain't right, if ya ask me, all this fussin' and fightin', 'specially with Mr. Leroy in the sickbed." She plucked J.T. out of Josie's arms, shaking her head over the obvious uproar in the household.

"Leroy and Inez are fighting?" Josie asked, clearly puzzled.

"Miz Inez is."

"How is Leroy?"

"That old fool's 'bout stubborn as a jackass. Doc says he's s'posed stay in bed and Mr. Alexander done throwed the biggest fit. Mighty glad I am that ya'll finally got here."

Chase noticed fierce emotions in Mattie's liquid brown eyes. She cared about the old man.

"Go on up, Miss Josie. You too," she said, giving Chase a motherly, no nonsense shove in the direction of the stairs. "That attorney's in the parlor out yonder. I'll go fetch him. Then me and J.T. will see about them cookies I baked this mornin'."

"Stanley's here?" Josie asked.

"Leroy called for him soon as he found out you was comin'."

An attorney? Chase didn't have a good feeling about this, but he went ahead and followed Josie up the stairs. In view of Mattie's forceful personality, he didn't figure he had much choice.

When they reached the upstairs landing, there was more than a little commotion. Inez's normally cold, controlled, Southern ladies do not get upset voice was raised and trembling. As if by prearrangement, Chase and Josie's steps slowed. There was no way to politely get out of eavesdropping short of turning around and hightailing it back down the stairs.

"What should we do?" Josie whispered.

"Walk slow?" he suggested.

Just then, Inez's voice raised even louder. "I'll not stand for this. Do you hear me? Your philandering thirty-something years ago was bad enough. I'll not have it thrown in my face after you're dead."

That bad feeling Chase had was growing by the second. Still, he couldn't help but think that was a low blow. He could hear Leroy's deeper voice, but he couldn't quite make out the words. Inez's, however, were quite clear.

"I will not allow you to do this, Leroy."

"Seems to me you don't got much choice." Leroy's voice was gaining strength. "You've had it your way for too long, madam. My attorneys know what to do now."

"Fine, then. I won't be staying around to watch you die." Another low blow, Chase thought. "I'm going home to Arkansas. My people are there and they certainly wouldn't dream of treating me in such a manner as this. I will *not* stay around and be the laughingstock of Louisiana because you've got some twisted sense of duty to a dead woman and her bastard son."

Chase pursed his lips in a silent whistle. He saw Josie glance at him and knew she was affronted on his behalf. Josie was that kind of lady.

"This house is yours," Leroy was saying.

"Do you think I want this dump? You haven't put a cent of your money into it in years. It's practically falling down around my feet!"

The place looked pretty good to Chase—if a person went in for opulence and showy art. It had the musty smell of old money. Very old money if there was any truth to the rumor about the fortune being dangerously skimpy.

"You have your own money, madam."

Did husbands really call their wives madam, Chase wondered. What a pity.

"Daddy didn't expect me to use my money for everyday living. And after what you've done to me, I wouldn't spend a dime of it on you."

Cold. Really cold.

"Then go home to Daddy."

They'd walked as slowly as they could. Now they were right upon the door to Leroy's room. Inez suddenly came rushing out and nearly collided with Chase. When she got a good look at him, Chase had the amused impression that she was about to succumb to a very old-fashioned fit of vapors. Then she sniffed and stuck her nose in the air as if she'd come upon a skunk, smack in the middle of her prissy hallway. Chase didn't figure anybody's spine could remain that rigid without snapping.

The hell of it was, not only did she snub him, she completely ignored Josie.

"Nice family," he muttered sarcastically.

She was obviously used to Inez's treatment, because she didn't even pause on her way to Leroy's side. Chase hung back, not sure what he was feeling now that the moment of confrontation was at hand.

The room was large. Although the decor had a pricey look to it, it was definitely a unisex room. There were no frills or noticeable perfumes to pique a man's imagination, to make him anticipate the joy of being invited in for pillow talk or erotic discoveries. Like his mother's bedroom had been. Like Josie's bedroom. Like his own.

Chase wondered if Leroy was aware of what he'd missed out on all these years.

Caught up in his own musings, he didn't realize that Josie had stepped back from Leroy's bedside, or that Leroy was studying him with narrow-eyed interest.

"Come on in here where I can see you, son."

Son. Chase's jaw clenched. It was an innocent enough term—he'd used it himself with J.T. Still, the name coming from Leroy's lips made his gut twist. His brain shouted flight, but his feet moved to do Leroy's bidding. Curiosity, he told himself.

Even with this latest stroke, Chase could tell that Leroy's mind was still sharp. Although his speech was slightly slurred and one side of his face drooped from partial paralysis, a keen sense of intelligence radiated from Leroy's pale blue eyes. Age and ill health couldn't disguise that he'd been a handsome man in his day. Had Sara Fowler been taken in by those good looks, Chase wondered.

"I suppose you know I'm dying, boy."

Josie gasped. "Leroy—"

Leroy's good hand lifted off the bed. Where his voice had been gruff, full of bluster at his rough announcement, it now softened. "Don't be kickin' up a fuss, sweet peach."

Sweet peach? The tender command in Leroy's voice along with the soft caring and love in his pale blue eyes gave Chase a glimpse of a very different man. A man, he realized, that Sara Fowler *could* have fallen in love with.

But where had that caring man been when Sara had needed him the most? The reminder set Chase back on track, hardening his features.

"You've got the look of your mama about you," Leroy said, turning his attention back to Chase.

"Did you call me all the way over here just to comment on my looks? A phone call would've done the job." Chase considered it a compliment that he looked like his mother. He despised the fact that he might have some of Leroy in him. He had little respect for the man who'd fathered him.

"Don't blame you none for being angry." Chase gave him points for astuteness. "All the same, you've done a mighty fine job with yourself."

"And I need to be getting back to that job. Is there a point here?" He saw the surprised look on Josie's face, heard her indrawn breath, and felt a twinge of guilt. He was acting little better than Inez had in the face of a dying man. But hell, what did she expect? For him to welcome his long-lost father with open arms? Thirty-two years of resentment could not vanish in a matter of minutes.

Leroy nodded as if he admired Chase's spunk. The little boy in him wanted that admiration. The man in him dismissed it.

"There is a point. Ain't no use kiddin' nobody. It's time I got my affairs in order. I've asked Stanley—my attorney—to explain the terms of my will."

"So what does that have to do with me?"

Leroy seemed at a loss for just a moment. "I figured you'd know about—"

"I do," Chase interrupted. He couldn't bring himself to say the words, *I know you're my father.*

"Then you're entitled to hear my instructions."

"You think I care about that?"

"I'm bettin' you do."

Chase felt everything within him tighten. He wanted to walk out, to tell Leroy exactly what he could do with his instructions, that he didn't want any part of him, just like Leroy hadn't wanted any part of Chase all those years ago. But Josie's pleading expression kept him rooted to the spot.

For her and her alone, he stayed, shifting to lean against the wall as Stanley Pinehurst came into the room. It was a dog and pony show as far as he was concerned.

Chase did his best to distance himself from the group. He couldn't make himself get too close to Leroy. Or to Josie. The look in her soft green eyes was bad enough. If she touched him in compassion, he'd probably give in to anything.

The attorney adjusted a pair of glasses on his nose and began reading. "I, Leroy Robert Alexander, being of sound mind..."

Chase couldn't believe that he was actually standing here, half listening to his biological father's wishes being spelled forth in legal terms. Did Leroy actually think he could buy Chase off? It just went to show that the man didn't know him at all.

No one *bought* Chase Fowler. If anything, *he* was the one who did the buying.

He didn't know whether it was morbid curiosity or the businessman in him that made him finally tune in to the attorney's droning voice.

"—half goes to Robert Troy Alexander or his issue," Pinehurst was saying. "In the event that Robert is deceased and there is no issue, the estate's assets, defined below, as aforementioned in section three, will become the legal property of Chase Lee Fowler, with the strict and unyielding stipulation that Chase Lee Fowler adopt and become legally known by his rightful surname of Alexander. In the event that these terms are not upheld, and there being no issue, the residual of the estate will resort in equal parts to assorted charities named hereafter..."

Josie's hand flew to her throat as Chase abruptly straightened from the wall. Leroy's stipulation was like a bomb exploding in the room, yet Chase's expression gave away nothing.

She wished she knew what he was thinking. Good Lord, she hadn't expected anything like this. Her stomach did a little flip when she realized what Leroy's contingency could mean. In essence, it would solve a part of her dilemma. Chase's name would be Alexander. Like hers. Like J.T.'s. No one would question the similarities in his and J.T.'s appearance.

Because he would be accepted as family.

She watched him carefully, trying not to hope too hard.

"Are we through?" Chase asked, his voice quietly controlled.

The attorney seemed a little caught off guard. "Basically...yes."

Chase nodded tersely, then to Josie's surprise, he simply turned and walked out.

Still stunned over Leroy's terms and Chase's lack of emotion, it was several seconds before Josie reacted. She gave Leroy's arm a comforting squeeze, then rushed after Chase. He was halfway to his truck when she caught up with him.

"Chase, wait."

He slowed, then turned. His blue eyes seemed to bore right through her. The look made her uneasy.

"Why did you walk out like that?" she asked, feeling her way in what clearly could turn into a minefield.

"Since I don't have any intention of honoring the terms of Leroy's will, I didn't see any point in staying."

"Chase, he's your father."

"I'm surprised he didn't ask for a blood test for proof positive."

Josie, too, found that interesting, especially because of who Leroy was, and for the number of years that had gone by. It made an odd sort of sense though, as she thought back on Inez and Leroy's relationship over the years—and that horrible exchange of words she and Chase had overheard. "He must have loved your mother."

"Did he? Then where was he all those years ago when she needed him? Or when I needed him? It's too late for reconciliations, Josie. I have a father. His name is James Fowler."

"But what about us?" she asked quietly.

"Us?"

"Me and J.T....and you."

"I don't see that anything's changed."

"Stanley said that if there's an heir—J.T.—that the inheritance will be split between the two of you."

"*If* my name becomes Alexander."

She didn't quite know how to have this conversation with him. Even to her own ears it sounded as if she were a vulture, just waiting for a man to die because there was money to be had. But that wasn't the case. She didn't care about the money for herself. It was her son's future and well-being that had her concerned.

"Would it be so bad?" she asked.

"What?"

"To take your birth father's name."

He frowned and pierced her with a steady gaze. "I could ask you the same thing."

"I don't understand."

"I, too, have a son who doesn't bear my name."

That was the point. A point that could make a world of difference in their lives. "But he could."

"On yours and Leroy's terms, you mean? I'm a Fowler, Josie, and I'm damned proud of it. After all James did for me and my mom, do you actually expect me to turn my back on him now? It would be like a slap in the face. James Fowler raised me as his own son. He loved me. He didn't have to, but he did. He's what a *real* father is all about." He swept his dark hair back off his forehead with an impatient hand.

"I'm proud of who I am," he repeated. "And I won't let Leroy or you or anyone else pressure me into being someone I'm not."

Josie admired his dedication to his father. Chase was an honorable man. But how long would it be before that innate honor caused him to push in a direction that would have far-reaching consequences? Because of his own birth circumstances, Chase had a strong belief in legitimacy and family ties—and honesty.

Her heart felt as if it were sitting in the pit of her stomach and her voice shook. "What about J.T.?"

"What about him?"

"Chase, he's not Bobby's biological son. If you don't go along with things, then J.T. has no rights, either."

"Are you trying to bribe me, Josie? Are you saying that you'll announce to the world that he's my son, but only if I go along with what Leroy wants?"

Josie instantly felt ashamed. She hung her head. "No."

"But you're afraid that I might spill the beans, is that it?"

She shook her head. The gesture could have been denial or uncertainty. At this point, she could barely think straight.

"I thought we were building something here, Josie. Trust at the very least."

"It's just that people would never understand."

"Does it really matter so much? Either way, J.T. is still Leroy's grandson."

"It's not that simple."

"I think it could be," he said quietly. "You set out to get pregnant four years ago and your motives were incredibly selfless. J.T. was your gift to Bobby. But Bobby's gone, Josie, and I'm not. Take my hand. Stand by my side."

Tears she hadn't been aware of welled up and spilled over her lashes. Yes, J.T. had been her gift to Bobby. The fact that Chase understood that so completely made her heart swell.

But Chase's acceptance could not stand up to or overcome the small-mindedness of an entire community. A community that might judge her son by an ignorant and unfair yardstick.

Her gaze swept over Chase, the strength of his body in jeans and a tight T-shirt, the sensuality of his full lips, the compassion and pain in his intense blue eyes. He was everything she could hope for in a man, yet she couldn't reach for and grasp the figurative hand he'd offered.

The distance between them was only a step, but it could have been a mile. They were operating on separate emotional levels, both born from two different paths in life that had somehow become intertwined.

They were bound together by destiny, yet torn apart by a secret.

"I'm not made of steel, Josie," he said when she didn't answer. "I do bleed."

"I know." She swallowed, trying to still the trembling in her voice. "I'm sorry."

"Then choose, sugar. You can either stay my brother's widow and live with your secrets, or you can come to me, openly, honestly. I know you're worried about the censure of the town, but we can face it together."

Josie had never felt so torn up in her life. If there was only herself to consider, the decision would be easy. But she couldn't bear the possibility of J.T. having to pay for her sins. "I can't," she whispered.

Silence seemed to stretch for an eon as he stared at her, as if he were memorizing everything about her. The muggy, August breeze rustled the leaves of the sycamore tree, carrying with it the distinct scent of the bayou.

It felt as if they stood there for hours, when in reality it was only seconds. Then he nodded once and gently touched her face, his fingertips so light she wondered if she'd imagined the caress. "Goodbye, Josie."

In an effort to hold back a scream, Josie swallowed repeatedly. Her heart felt shattered, rent apart by a despair that went too deep for repair. Through a sheen of tears, she watched him walk to his pickup. Not even with Bobby's death had she suffered such incredible sadness.

The taillights of his truck were no longer visible when Josie finally went back in the house to collect J.T. Her son came barreling through the parlor with Mattie on his heels. Automatically, she stooped to pick him up.

She buried her face in his silky dark hair and simply stood there, holding him as if the strength of her arms alone could protect him.

She'd just made a major decision on his behalf, and for the life of her she honestly didn't know if it had been the right one. To keep her silence would secure her son's future in this town.

But at the expense of what?

Everything within her felt as if it had shut down. She told herself to turn, to walk to the door, to function, but the buzzing in her ears obliterated all else. She felt light-headed. She couldn't face the caring look on Mattie's face, nor answer the maid's concerned inquiry. Without a glance for Mattie or anyone else who might have been looking, she gathered up her purse and walked out the door.

Her world had finally, truly shattered.

Chapter Fourteen

It had been a hellish week since he'd left the Alexander's house. And Josie. A week full of anticipation and disappointment and emotions that vacillated between hope, despair, anger and resignation.

He couldn't go on like this, living on the edge, being so close, yet so far from the one woman who'd made such an impact on his life.

It was times like this that he needed the stability and comfort of home.

Chase buzzed the farmhouse in Rayville twice, dipped his wings in acknowledgment of his father's wave and aimed the Cessna for the airstrip behind the back pasture. By the time he'd landed and secured the single-engine plane, James Fowler's pickup was pulling up on the runway amid a cloud of dust.

In deference to the heat, James's chest was bare under a pair of baggy overalls. He was a giant of a man, standing six foot six, with freckled skin and wavy red hair. There wasn't a lick of resemblance between the two men, but Chase didn't give a darn. He'd take on anyone who dared to make a comment. Looks were superficial. No matter what,

James Fowler was his father in every sense of the word except one.

"Hi, Dad." Instead of the traditionally masculine hand shake, the two men embraced.

James stepped back, scrutinizing Chase much like a hen would her chicks. "Well, son, you look like you've been put through the ringer backwards. Work's keeping you busy, huh?"

Son. Coming from James Fowler, it felt right. Damned good. "Work's fine." Chase grinned even though his heart wasn't in it. "Life's the pits, though."

"Figured something was up when you called."

"You mean I can't call my old man unless something's up?"

"You know better than that. Let's go on up to the house where it's cool. We'll have a beer and solve the world's problems."

"Sounds good." They'd spent countless hours together, just like this, talking, teaching, listening. Whether they were tinkering with airplanes or plowing fields or kicking back after supper, the rock-steadiness James Fowler exuded always brought Chase a sense of balance.

They entered the white clapboard house through the kitchen door and already Chase felt calmer. Just being home did that to him.

At first, after his mother's death, it had been hard sitting in this kitchen, which had been his mother's domain. It was as if he'd expected his welcome to suddenly vanish. But James had soon set him straight. There were no secrets between the two men, no conflicts or uncertainties left unresolved.

Just a steady, unconditional love.

"You want to tell me about it?" James's soft-spoken words broke into Chase's musing.

He took a swig of beer and set the can back on the wood table, idly rubbing his finger over the three sets of initials that were carved into the table's surface.

It had been the day after the adoption that he'd scraped his initials in the table, not out of a malicious attempt to deface or destroy, but as a childish affirmation that he finally belonged. James had walked in just as he'd finished and Chase had been horrified, terrified that the man would reprimand him for doing something stupid. The scared little boy in him had been sure that James would "unadopt" him.

Instead, James had studied the initials—C.L.F.— and nodded in approval. Then to Chase's astonishment, James had picked up the blunt tool and set about carving his own and Sara's initials just under Chase's, saying he reckoned they ought to start a family tradition right there at the breakfast table. It'd be a Fowler heirloom.

By rights, J.T.'s initials should be on this table, too.

"I have a son," Chase blurted.

Both of James's red eyebrows rose. "Well, now, I always wanted to be a grandpa. Sort of thought I'd get a daughter-in-law first, though."

"I'm not real sure if I can swing that one." He closed his eyes for just a minute, feeling something close to despair settle in the pit of his stomach. Love wasn't supposed to hurt this way. "Are you disappointed in me?"

"Son, you couldn't disappoint me if you tried. It must be something mighty big eating at you for you to even suggest such a thing." James reached over and clasped Chase on the shoulder. "Get it all out now, Chase."

Chase grinned. "You know, I've always figured there wasn't anything you couldn't fix."

"Now don't go shoving me up on no pedestals," James said gruffly.

For some, ridiculously unaccountable reason, Chase felt his eyes sting. "I love you, Dad."

"I know, son. And I love you."

Chase chugged half the can of beer in an effort to swallow his emotions. "His name is James. J.T. for short."

"Hell of a good name. Hell of a coincidence, too." James made the last statement sound like a question.

"Yeah. It had to be coincidence or destiny or something. At the time, Josie didn't even know *my* name."

"Yikes."

"Exactly. It's all tied up with the Alexanders..." Chase told his father everything. They drank beer and talked, ate dinner and talked some more. Night fell and the temperature cooled pleasantly, so they moved onto the porch, content in each other's company, lulled by the familiar sounds of farm animals and an old barn owl. A harvest moon hung low in the sky like a big yellow ball.

"How did you handle the talk, Dad?" Rayville was a small town, just like Alexander. Marrying what some folks would call a fallen woman and taking on her bastard son couldn't have been easy.

"Gossip's for mean-spirited people. I loved your mama and she loved me and we both loved you.

Family was important to us, so we mostly did stuff together and didn't worry about whether or not we'd fit in socially."

"And that was it?"

"Pretty much. The happiness the three of us felt sort of rubbed off on folks. Besides, I think what you're remembering is the insults you viewed through a child's eyes. Children are just little people trying to find their place in the world. Any meanness you ran into was probably from other little kids. As an adult, you learn forgiveness. The folks who really matter will stand by you."

"I believe that. But I just don't know how to make Josie see it."

"Give her some time, son. She's got a lot on her plate right now. She sounds real special and I'm sure she'll come around. And if she don't, well, hell, send her on over to me." James winked. "I'll tell her what a good catch you are."

Chase laughed, feeling at ease for the first time in almost a week. "I just might do that."

"Mind if I give you another little piece of advice?"

"Hell, no. Advise away."

"Make peace with your past, son."

His easy feeling disappeared. Chase started to shake his head.

"Hear me out, now." He waited until Chase gave him his full attention. "You've got a lot of unanswered questions swimming around in your head. No sense in letting them fester. Ask your questions, Chase. Listen to the answers you get with an open mind, then let it go and find forgiveness. Everybody's got their own reasons for making the choices they do. Might not go along with what you'd do under the same circumstances, but you've got to remember that it wasn't *your* choice to begin with. You hear what I'm saying to you?''

"I hear what you're saying, but..." Chase leaned forward and braced his elbows on his knees. "Why are you taking his side, Dad? Leroy didn't seem to give a damn about you when he blithely demanded I drop your name and take on his."

"I'm not threatened by that, son. A name's just a few letters that make a noise when you say them. It's what's in the heart that counts. It don't matter what your last name is, or little J.T.'s for that matter. You're my son and nothing or nobody can ever change that."

Chase looked at James, his admiration so great he could hardly contain it, much less put it into words. "You know what? I'm so glad Mom had the good sense to fall in love with you. You're one hell of a man."

JOSIE SAT at Leroy's bedside, bringing him up to date on the progress Harold was making with the new irrigation system. It was several minutes before she realized she'd lost his attention.

When she followed the direction of his gaze, she nearly toppled out of the chair. Her heart gave a sharp, deep thud, then began to race, sending a flash of heat over her tightened skin. She was suddenly swamped with a light-headed exhilaration that made her feel slightly faint.

Chase stood in the open doorway, radiating strength and a provocative sexuality that had little to do with swagger and a lot to do with his innate confidence as a man. Just looking at him created a rush of excitement in the pit of her stomach.

She told herself to look away, to stop this insane torture, but her mind refused to obey.

Lord, how she missed his touch, his smile, the erotic rasp of his voice as he'd admire a particular part of her body, or state his intentions to have her his way. She missed the strength of his arms around her, not only in pleasure, but during the quiet times, times that bespoke of a deep and growing friendship.

Seeing him now just magnified the misery she'd experienced over the past week. Even J.T., it seemed, had joined forces against her; he'd been uncharacteristically difficult to handle. Her son had taken up whining as a new hobby and every other word that came out of his mouth had something to do with Chase.

She wished to God there was a way around this heartache. But too many people counted on her to be perfect. To reach out to Chase would create a hornet's nest of stinging repercussions. If she had any doubts, all she had to do was look at the treatment Lindsey Wakefield and her children received from the good citizens of Alexander, Louisiana.

Chase's deep voice put a halt to her introspection.

"Mattie told me to come up." His words were directed to Leroy, but his penetrating gaze was still on Josie.

"Well, then, don't just stand there, boy. There's plenty of chairs in this room. Might as well occupy one."

Josie stood and fumbled with the hem of her cotton skirt. She didn't think she could remain in this room without doing something foolish. Like bursting into tears over what couldn't be. "The two of you would probably like some privacy. I'd better go."

"Stay," Chase said quietly. "Please."

An emotion very much like need flashed in his eyes for just an instant. That he exuded such strength and confidence made the vulnerability all the more difficult to resist. It just wasn't in her to deny him. She nodded and sat back down.

Chase moved slowly into the room. He saw the desire and pain and longing in Josie's eyes. It gave him hope. But like his dad had told him, he needed to clear up the voids in his past before he could move on with his future.

"You made a decision yet?" Leroy asked.

Chase sat in the vacant chair by Leroy's bed and propped his booted ankle on his knee. He spared a quick glance at Josie, then turned his attention to the man who could give him the answers he needed.

"I think you already know my decision," Chase said. Leroy Alexander hadn't gotten where he was today without being a fairly astute judge of character.

Leroy nodded. "I wasn't tryin' to railroad you."

"Weren't you?" Chase asked softly.

"All right. I suppose I figured it was worth a try."

"I don't intimidate or bend under pressure."

"I suspected that about you. You're a lot like me, you know."

Chase had to make a conscious effort to relax his jaw. Steadily, he held the other man's gaze.

Leroy was the first to look away. He sighed and gripped the edge of the blanket with a fist that no longer carried any strength. "I suppose you've got some questions."

"A few."

"Well, spit 'em out. I ain't no mind reader."

Chase's eyes narrowed. "Why don't we start at the beginning. With my mother."

"Sara." Leroy said the name with a reverence that made Chase want to deck him, regardless of the man's state of health. Thankfully, he took himself in hand.

"It was just after I'd married Inez that I met Sara." A look of sadness filled Leroy's pale eyes, but Chase was determined to remain hardened. "She was full of kindness and serenity, with a beauty that darn near took my breath away. She made me feel like a man." Leroy shut his eyes for an instant.

"That might sound foolish, but you'd have to know my wife to understand why I had to have Sara, what it meant to have a girl look at me like the sun came up in the mornin' and went down at night just for my benefit." He paused and drew in a breath. "I didn't tell her I was married."

Chase swore. He glanced at Josie. She looked as if she couldn't decide whether to hug Leroy to her breast or clobber him for his insensitivity.

"When Inez got wind of the affair, all hell broke loose. She threatened to ruin me, and at the time she had the power to do it."

Money. By God, it always came down to money. "Did you know my mother was pregnant with me?"

"Yes."

Chase felt like shouting, but he kept his calm. The thought of his mother—scared, alone and pregnant—did not endear him to the sick old man in the bed. "Where the hell was your duty, sir? Your duty to my mother?"

"Nowhere in sight, it seems." Leroy's shoulders hunched in, making him appear small. Regret colored his features, but it was too late for regrets as far as Chase was concerned. There was too much water under the bridge.

"By that time, Inez was pregnant, too."

Chase was starting to sorely regret this visit. He had a knot the size of a piston in his stomach. Good old daddy had been sleeping with both women at the same time.

"I had to choose," Leroy said, his voice weak.

That statement hurt. It shouldn't have, but it did. How could a parent actually choose between his kids? Then again, Leroy wasn't anywhere near Chase's definition of a parent. He glanced once more at Josie. She, too, seemed to be having trouble with the concept of Leroy's callous explanation.

"So you abandoned my mother because she wasn't from the right background, is that it?"

"I sent money."

Chase's lip curled up in a sneer. "Obviously not enough to insure proper medical attention."

"She sent the money back. I don't expect you to understand the way things have got to be around here, son, but upholding the Alexander name has always had to come first."

"You'd be surprised how well I understand that." He said the words to Leroy, but his eyes were locked with Josie's. The flash of shame in her green eyes made him regret the barb. Damn that good ol' family name. "If Bobby hadn't passed on, would we be having this conversation?"

Leroy shrugged one shoulder. At the mention of his other son—the legitimate one—his eyes became misty. "I'd like to think we would, but I can't honestly say."

He had to give Leroy points for frankness. The fact that Chase was secure in the love of his own family took a lot of the sting out of Leroy's rejection.

"Aren't there such things as bone marrow transplants?" Chase asked.

Josie gripped the arms of the Victorian, brocade chair. This conversation had to be costing Chase, but he kept his emotions well hidden. She hurt for the little boy in him who'd been dismissed because in the hierarchy of a small town, he hadn't been good enough.

It made her question her own loyalty to that protocol.

Especially now that he'd asked a question she hadn't even thought about before. My God. If Leroy had known about Chase, why hadn't he been on the phone the second they'd found out about Bobby's leukemia?

"If you cared so much for my brother, why didn't you come to me? I might have been his best hope for survival."

Josie, too, wanted to know the answer to that. She remembered practically the whole town being tested as possible donors. They'd even entered Bobby into the national computers in search of a compatible match.

She looked at her father-in-law, waiting for him to answer, keeping a tenuous hold on the anger simmering just below the surface of her carefully masked outrage.

"We had a whole mess of people tested," Leroy hedged, clearly uneasy.

"But not me."

"No."

"Why not?" Chase demanded.

"Inez was dead set against it."

"What?" Josie came up out of the chair, too stunned to sit.

Leroy looked at her with genuine sorrow. "I don't know if I was tryin' to atone to the woman or what, but to my bitter regret, I bowed to Inez's histrionics and demands."

"How could you?" Josie paced away from the bed, distancing herself from the horror of the possibility of Bobby's wasted death.

"You know as well as I that Bobby had a rare type of bone marrow. Inez insisted that if they couldn't find a match in the nationwide computers, a half brother would hardly be a possibility."

Josie's already low opinion of her mother-in-law died a final death. As did her opinion of Leroy. Her hands shook and her voice trembled, her stomach twisted tighter than a bobbin of silk thread. Who *were* these people? No one had a right to play God with another person's life. Bobby's life.

"I was Bobby's wife. That should have been *my* decision. Not Inez's. Or yours, Leroy. You should have told me."

Chase stood up, his gaze on Josie. She was a tough lady. The way her hands fisted at her sides told him she was making every effort to fight her emotions.

But the single tear that slipped from the corner of her eye betrayed her.

He didn't care how it looked to anyone. Josie needed a pair of arms around her. Moving to her side, he gently touched her shoulder, then gathered her close. He admired her devotion to the brother he'd never known. He was strong enough not to let her past feelings for another man—a good man—bother him now.

They stood together for a moment, reliving a loss that might have been prevented.

Chase pitied Inez, a frigid woman who'd refused to bend—even at the expense of her son's life. He also pitied Leroy. The almighty dollar and the lure of power had turned him into a lonely old man. Leroy had made the only choices he could based on who he was.

His father's words echoed in his mind, and suddenly Chase felt a spreading sense of peace. Josie, too, could benefit from those words.

"Regrets only muddy things up, sugar. What's done, can't be undone. Now's the time for forgiveness." He placed a gentle kiss against her temple, then went once more to stand by Leroy's bed.

"I can't be the son you lost, sir, which seems to be your motive behind putting me in your will. The choices you made thirty-two years ago were right for you...and as it turns out, they were pretty damn good for me, too. James Fowler's been the only father I've known. I could never dishonor or discount his love by replacing his name with yours. I'd just as soon not have any bad feelings between the two of us, though. You're tough as nails, and I don't think you're quite ready to meet your maker. Maybe sometime soon we can establish a sort of friendship.''

Leroy nodded. ''I don't suppose I deserve it, but that'd be good.''

Josie had her back to them, her hands gripping her elbows as if she'd turned in on herself. On his way out the door, Chase stopped in front of her, placing his finger under her chin so she'd look at him.

''Make your peace with him, sugar. You're probably the one person in this world that he truly cares about.''

''I know,'' she whispered.

''Will you come to me, then?''

Her green eyes pleaded for understanding. ''I need some time, Chase. My whole world has suddenly shifted. I've got to make some sense of it.''

''I'll wait.''

Chapter Fifteen

After Chase left, Josie took a walk around the gardens, trying to give herself some time, some balance. She didn't trust herself to face Leroy just yet.

She'd wanted Chase to see the good, gentle side of Leroy's nature. Instead, she'd had a shocking glimpse of the controlling, arrogant side of her father-in-law. The side she'd so adamantly defended over the years as simply being his business personality, a front.

It gave her one hell of a dose of reality.

How long did she owe allegiance to a family—or a name—who didn't think she was significant enough, even as Bobby's wife, to make important decisions?

There were no guarantees that Chase's bone marrow would have been a match for Bobby, but even if there had been a remote possibility, it should have been considered.

Chase had realized that. Even though he hadn't known his brother, even though he had bad feelings toward the family, he wouldn't have hesitated a second if there was a chance he could save a life.

He was that type of man.

He wasn't shallow. He didn't place money and social standing above love and loyalty. He'd proven that by openly showing pride in his adoptive father's name.

And that basic confidence so inherent in Chase was contagious, Josie realized.

She thought back to how he made her feel when she was in his arms, as if she could be anyone she wanted, without the need to present a good front or worry about the opinions of others.

Chase had been taught some good lessons in life. He had a capacity for love that a woman—or a little boy—would be fortunate to be the recipient of.

She wanted to be on the receiving end of that love. By heavens, she deserved it. Just thinking the phrase gave her strength.

For too long she'd stood in the shadows, worried over saying the right thing, doing the right thing, being good enough. It was a stupid, senseless, wimpy way to live. Money, reputation, a fancy name—what did it all mean?

Nothing, she answered herself, coming to a sudden decision. Nothing at all without love.

The step she was about to take was a heck of a gamble, but it felt right. First, though, she needed to clear the air with Leroy.

She headed back inside the house with a great deal of purpose. Leroy seemed to sense the new, determined, confident air about her.

"I can't undo what I've done," he said before she had a chance to speak.

"No, you can't. But perhaps you've done me a favor."

"How so?"

"The decision you made about Bobby's life wasn't fair to me. But out of respect and love, I intend to afford you a courtesy you didn't think to extend to me. You can't make Chase come around to your way of thinking, so I imagine you'll be making some changes in your wishes. To that end, there's something else you ought to know."

"Missy, you can't—"

Josie held up her hand. "Listen to me, Leroy. Because if you don't, you're bound to hear about it from somebody else." She took a deep breath. "J.T. is not Bobby's child."

He seemed too stunned for speech. A shadow of the arrogant, lord-of-the-manor countenance swept his features. It was just the sort of judgmental, censoring reaction she'd worried over. Strangely enough, it didn't have the impact she thought it would.

"You stepped out on my son?"

"Yes. In a manner of speaking."

"What the hell other manner is there, I'd like to know?"

"Don't try to intimidate me, Leroy. I'm past that. Besides, you're not exactly in a position to throw stones."

They say that age mellows a person. It must be true, Josie thought, because Leroy let out a deep sigh and reached for her hand. "You're right, sweet peach. It don't matter no how. That boy's still my grandson. Nobody's got to know any different."

"You're right. He *is* your grandson. But people *are* going to know. Leroy, J.T. is Chase's son."

SEVERAL HOURS LATER, Josie pulled up in front of the newspaper office on main street. What she was about to do was a gift to Chase. Whether he wanted her in the bargain was up to him. The gift she wanted to give him came with no strings attached.

By tomorrow morning the whole town, and anyone who cared to research it in the future, would know that Chase Lee Fowler was J.T.'s father.

The office was noisy and smelled of paper and ink. Phones rang incessantly and computer keys clicked. Josie paused just inside the door and took a fortifying breath.

She saw Gracie Jones seated at a cluttered desk in the back of the room. She'd gone to school with Gracie and she admired her, both as a woman and as a journalist.

Five years ago, Gracie had lost her husband to cancer. Some speculated that his death had been premature and by his own hand—and that Gracie had assisted him. It had created quite a stir in town.

Suddenly, the gamble Josie was about to take didn't feel quite so risky. This woman had been through heartaches, suffered greatly through loss and dealt with nasty gossips. She was a woman who knew about sacrifices. If anybody could write Josie's story like it ought to be written, Gracie would be the one.

Josie stepped past the glass partition and stopped in front of Gracie's desk. "Gracie?"

Distracted, the other woman looked up. "Josie! It's good to see you. What brings you to our chaotic newsroom?"

She clutched her purse to her lap and slowly sat down. "I've got a story for you."

Gracie automatically picked up a pad and pencil. She was a beautiful woman with an uncanny knack of seeing not only the surface of a person or event, but the deep, hidden heart that would be missed by someone less intuitive. "What kind of story?" she asked gently.

Josie thought about it for a moment. "I guess you could say it's a human interest story...."

JOSIE HAD TEARS in her eyes the next morning as she finished reading the newspaper. With her special brand of sensitivity, Gracie had handled the subject in a manner that was incredibly touching. In part—because of Leroy's ill health—the article was a tribute to the Alexanders, an unfolding story about the founders of the town and their family successors. A history of sorts.

The piece about Bobby's bout with leukemia was especially poignant. Gracie gave an account of the desperate emotions of a dying man's wife, and the beautiful sacrifice both Josie and Chase had made in order to give Bobby the child he so wanted.

The article inferred that it was a mutual decision between the brother of a dying man and his brother's wife.

Although it wasn't the way Josie had told the story to Gracie, the encounter had been romanticized as being planned.

Gracie had labeled it an act of love.

It was beautifully written. And so very touching.

Josie swiped at the tears on her cheeks and got up to pour a cup of coffee. She was staring out the kitchen window when Chase's truck pulled up the lane.

He'd asked her to come to him—which she'd planned to do. So why was he here instead? Had he read the article? Lord, she wasn't prepared.

She looked down at her matte satin boxer pajamas. They were presentable enough, but still, she felt vulnerable, caught off guard. She wasn't dressed and her hair was probably a mess. But it was too late to do anything about her appearance.

Running her fingers through her unbound hair, Josie went to the door.

Now that she was no longer burdened by a secret, she felt scared and nervous, as if she were seeing Chase for the first time. Her heart slammed up against her ribs and for some ridiculous reason, she was having trouble drawing a steady breath.

He wore a pair of dark blue dress jeans and a white button-down shirt that hugged his masculine frame as if tailor-made. He didn't look like a man who had any plans for spending a long day in the cockpit of a crop duster. He could have been dressed for gentle courting or hot seduction. In either case, the aggressive set of his shoulders told her he'd be a success at any course he chose.

"Can I come in?" he asked.

Josie realized she'd been clutching the edge of the door as if she were about to slam it shut. She stepped back and motioned him in. "Of course."

For some reason, she'd expected him to touch her, or at the very least, strike up a conversation. Callers normally stated their business right away. But Chase simply moved into the room ahead of her, not saying a word. He seemed unusually restless, like a man with a great weight on his mind. She saw him hesitate, then lift a framed picture of J.T. off the mantel. He studied the photograph then placed it back on the wood and turned to her.

"Chase, I—"

"Don't talk, sugar. I've been rehearsing this pretty little speech in my head all morning and if I don't get it out, I'm liable to go nuts."

Josie's stomach gave an odd lurch. The intensity in his voice and eyes made her nervous. She pinched the edges of her pajama shorts in her fingers, worrying the silky fabric. She did as he asked and remained silent.

"I told you I'd wait, give you some time, but I can't. The truth of the matter is, I love you. I'll take you any way I can get you."

He loved her? "Chase—"

"No," he interrupted. "Just listen. You could have met somebody after Bobby died, married him and he'd have simply been a stepfather to J.T. But because it's me, because you *know* that I'm the boy's father, it makes it a whole different crop of cotton for you."

She opened her mouth—at least to comment on his declaration of love—but closed it again as he just plowed forward.

"Pride's a fine thing, sugar, but it's damned lonely. Marry me. Please. J.T.'s paternity will just be between me and you. I swear to God."

"No."

"Damn it, Josie. Can you stand there and tell me you don't love me?"

"No."

"No, what?"

"No, I can't stand here and tell you I don't love you. I *do* love you. With all my heart. I think I've loved you since that night at the motel when you said in that lazy drawl of yours, 'Tell me what you want, sugar.' You didn't judge me, Chase, not then, not when you came to town and found out about us, and not now."

She hadn't realized that her feet had carried her across the room. Without recalling how she'd gotten there, Josie found herself in front of Chase, her palm resting against the warmth of his chest radiating through his shirt.

He raised his brow and a slow grin crossed his lips. "Well...I did have a few doubts in the beginning."

"But you asked your questions and accepted my answers."

His hand covered the back of hers against his chest. "Maybe because I wanted another opportunity to look at your lingerie."

Josie smiled. The way his eyes traveled over her scanty pajamas made her nipples pebble. They pressed against the thin satin in a prominent display of her emotions. "Do you really want to marry me? Because if this is just about J.T.—"

He placed his finger against her lips. "God knows I love that little kid. But I love his mother, too." The pad of his thumb slipped over her lips. "I want to see your sexy lingerie strewn around my bedroom, your perfume bottles lined up on my dresser. I want your face to be the first one I see in the morning and the last at night. So what do you say, sugar. Will you marry me?"

The satin boxers created little barrier between them, especially since she was naked beneath the silky covering. She felt the press of his hips, the hard length of his arousal as he pulled her lower body against his. Had she not already made up her mind, this would have constituted unfair play.

"Yes," she whispered.

His head dipped as he claimed her lips. He wrapped his arms around her and held her with an overwhelmingly gentle strength that lifted her feet from the floor.

Like lovers renewing their vows after a long separation, they tasted and touched and sighed out their pleasure. With her fingers tangled in his dark hair, she buried her face in his neck and placed soft, openmouthed kisses along his throat and earlobe and jaw. Traces of his cologne clung to her lips and tongue.

Slowly, allowing her to savor every inch of friction, he set her back on her feet.

"About J.T. . . . ." she began.

"Shh," he murmured. "It's not important. My dad said a name's just a few letters that make a sound when you say them. It's what's in the heart that counts."

Josie pulled back to look at him. "Your dad sounds like a wise man."

"He is. He even offered to plead my case with you." His hands made soft sweeps along her ribs and the sides of her breasts, each pass pulling her satin top a little higher. "He figures I'm a pretty good catch."

"No need to do any pleading. J.T. and I both agree." His fingers were at the edge of her pajama top, toying with the top button. Oh, how she loved his hands, his body, all the facets of him that made up the whole man. "J.T. is lucky to have you for a dad."

Something like sadness flickered in his eyes for a split instant. Josie placed her hands over his to stop their wandering. Could he think . . . ?

"Chase, did you by any chance read the paper this morning?"

"Sugar, I'm trying my level best to figure out a way to get you in the bedroom and you want to talk about the news?"

Josie disengaged herself from his arms and picked up the paper from the table. "I think you'd better read this."

One of his dark brows cocked, but he accepted the newspaper. Her heart pounded and her palms began to sweat. Would he view this as she'd intended? As a gift of her love? After all, her decision to go to the paper not only put her life in the limelight, it also bared Chase for public scrutiny.

She watched him carefully, breath held.

At last he looked up. His deep blue eyes were bright, filled with incredible tenderness and love.

"Well?" she asked, the suspense nearly causing her to faint.

He opened his arms and Josie stepped into them. With his lips pressed to her hair, he held her tightly.

"I gotta tell you, sugar, when you set your mind to doing something, you do it in a big way." He kissed her with a gentleness that nearly melted her bones. "You know we're going to take some flak over this."

"Probably."

"I swear to God I won't let anybody hurt you or J.T. As soon as it can be arranged, we'll be married. I'll see to it that you become the first lady of Alexander, Louisiana, make sure that you never forget that you belong, that you deserve all the success and happiness you could possibly hope to gather in one lifetime."

"Chase, I already know that. I love you. We're all that matters now."

She rose on tiptoe and initiated a kiss so fiery he could have sworn his heart stopped for a moment.

"Is J.T. still asleep?" he asked, making a manly effort to control his breathing.

"Yes. He'll probably be out for another hour or so."

His hands went to work on the buttons of her pajama top. "I don't suppose I could interest you in a trial run for the honeymoon? Just so we get it right, you understand."

"Absolutely." She grabbed his hand and led him down the hall toward the bedroom.

"I love a woman who takes charge."

Josie gave him a secretive smile that caused his heart to thud against his ribs. "What's your favorite color?" she asked, the tip of her tongue playing erotically over her pouty bottom lip.

"Red."

"Then you're in luck. I just happen to have a couple of red scarves . . . and a four-poster bed."

Chase laughed, feeling as if he were indeed the luckiest man alive. She was a wickedly seductive woman, all his wildest and softest dreams wrapped up in one incredibly beautiful package. And by God, at long last she was his.

Epilogue

James Troy Alexander-Fowler tried his best to keep from fidgeting in the hard plastic chair in his Sunday School room. He folded his hands and bowed his head like Mouse said to do.

Today he'd get to go into the big church with Mama and Daddy so Brother Mac could pray over Cassandra. He figured it was pretty neat having a sister, 'cept she was kinda small in his opinion. She'd been born now for three months—Daddy had reminded him that just this morning—and he hadn't even gotten a chance to practice his sharing, which he had to admit he was pretty proud of. It was just that her hands were so little she couldn't hold his trucks when he tried to do that big brother stuff and be sweet.

He squeezed his eyes shut real tight. He probably ought to be listening to the prayer Mouse was saying, but his mind was awfully busy this Sunday morning.

They lived in the big house on the hill now, the one where the airplanes were. He got to fly in those planes with Daddy now, and that was superneat.

Mama bought Aunt Dottie's store and sold lots of ladies underwear and nightgowns. Even Grandma Halliday helped out with the sewing. Mama said Daddy must have charmed Grandma or something, cuz she didn't take to pickin' on people anymore.

When Mouse said "Amen," J.T. felt a little guilty cuz he hadn't been listening when they were talking to God. Maybe God wouldn't notice that he hadn't been paying attention.

When he opened his eyes, he felt happiness tickle his tummy. Daddy was standing at the doorway, looking just like a daddy ought to in his fancy church clothes. Without waiting to be excused, J.T. hopped right up, and sort of forgot he wasn't supposed to run in class.

Daddy didn't fuss, though. He just grinned. "You ready to go into the big church and watch Cassey get sprinkled with water?"

"Yep." He took his daddy's hand as they walked from the Sunday School rooms toward the sanctuary. "Is Cassey gonna cry when they get her wet?"

"She might."

J.T. thought about that. "But she won't be sad, will she?"

"Gee, I hope not, son. Remember your mama told us it was our job as the boys of the household to make sure the girls didn't ever get sad."

J.T. nodded his head solemnly. He took his duties as big brother seriously. "I could kiss her and make it better," he suggested.

"Well, now, there's an idea. I bet it'd do the trick."

"Or we could write her name on the table. That would make her all better."

"Think so?"

"Yep." He still couldn't believe Daddy had let him write on the furniture. But Grandpa Jim had brought the table over in the pickup after the wedding, and before Mama could even dust it off good, Daddy had let him write the letters of his name, right smack on the top of the thing. Daddy said it was a tradition. Mama even got to do it, too.

There were a whole bunch of people in the church. Grandpa Leroy in his wheelchair—Daddy said he was a tough old cuss who'd probably outlive all of them—sat smack dab in the middle of the aisle. Grandpa Jim sat next to Grandma and Grandpa Halliday. J.T. shook his head. Sometimes he forgot and called one of the grandpas the wrong thing. Big families were tough on a kid.

He saw Aunt Dottie—who had finally up and married old Mr. Potts—and Mary Alice and Bud and Gracie Jones.

Everybody was smiling and hugging and makin' a fuss. It was kinda yucky to get kissed on so much. He started to make a face, but Daddy beat him to it, which was kind of bad of him because J.T. felt an attack of the giggles coming on.

The tickle slipped out in a laugh that was louder than he'd expected.

Mama stopped talking to the lady with blue hair and turned around, holding Cassandra in a fluffy blanket. She was prettier than most moms. Daddy even said so.

All the townspeople sort of stepped aside with mushy looks on their faces, and everybody watched as she walked down the aisle toward Daddy and him.

Even though he was little, J.T. realized there was something extra special between his parents. Since they got married, Mama smiled all the time.

J.T. smiled, too. He had Chase for a daddy and lots of airplanes to play around and a new baby sister—even though she didn't know how to play yet. Yeah, J.T. figured, God did a real good job in the prayers and wishes department.